T0003384

Naked Light and the Blind Eye

Sanya Osha

Langaa Research & Publishing CIG
Mankon, Bamenda

Publisher:
Langaa RPCIG
Langaa Research & Publishing Common Initiative Group
P.O. Box 902 Mankon
Bamenda
North West Region
Cameroon
Langaagrp@gmail.com
www.langaa-rpcig.net

Distributed in and outside N. America by African Books Collective
orders@africanbookscollective.com
www.africanbookscollective.com

ISBN-10: 9956-764-20-5

ISBN-13: 978-9956-764-20-4

First published by Future Fiction London in 2010

Part I

The window panes had a sombre cast as rain streaked down them like half frozen tears. Night time didn't seem persuasive. It was as if it didn't believe in itself. The only truly convincing aspect about it appeared to be its awareness of other beings, other entities that strode through the dusky somnolence. And in the rain-soaked evening, some people, bricklayers were hammering away upon iron rods. The fever of commerce had reached its highest peak. Steely clanks chimed on incessantly until it clutched the root of the teeth and more distressingly the spirit.

She had gone. Just like that. But that wasn't what bothered me in the immediate sense. I touched the sad window panes and tears welled within me and then ended up like locks at the back of my throat. As I stood looking down below at the slow moving traffic and the disturbed array of flashlights on the rain-swept street, I wanted to bring out an eye, cold and artificial, I wanted to draw it a hair's breadth from the pane so that it could catch the chill that had frozen my soul. My being in its entirety blended with the rain that was making slow water noises. The rain caught a green hue and streaked on and my soul sank deep with it. It was the sadness of the rain that brought back to me what I consider the origins of my fucked-upness. I felt so twisted and incapable of turning around my life. My seasons had seen the merriment of the sun but had now forgotten what it seemed like to be favoured. My accursed state seemed to bear me like an ocean against whose currents I am powerless to turn. So down I go, fucked-up by the curse of the sun. I'm almost sixty now and night is the breeze I see before me.

It hadn't been like this for me as a young man. I had plans. And I also had ideals. After several hesitations I had resolved to be a word, and like every word that passes from mouth to mouth, I wanted to move from my etymological locus through one age to another, gathering different meanings and usages until I realised at least the limits of my boundaries and then invented for myself possibilities beyond my immediate range. I had hoped to be a whole race, an infant, a grown male (which is what I actually am), a grown female pulling through a gamut of experiences and manifestations along the way.

Sometimes I had hoped to deliberately refuse to shift my myriad social interactions to enjoy the beauties of ambiguity, the sole mystery behind the thoroughly poeticised experience. Lyricism immediately connotes the fluidity of oceans and rivers. It celebrates the labyrinthine mazes of meaning. The supreme feminine form that undresses itself with perfumes in a nocturnal continent of satin was the ultimate image that I pursued. This was my ambition, *to be*, beyond the frustrations and abuses of a stark reality that bleeds the language of life, of its mobility, and then eventually robs it of all poetry. Otherwise, like some old man smoking a pipe at the edge of a derelict town, I had hoped to make attempts to select, to weed out presences and influences that undermined the language which activated the profusions of my meaning. The desiccated word that I had intended to nurse would have freed me and that would have become the relic of a defeated culture. This relic of ana word was nothing but the death of an entire civilisation. A word that didn't just lose its connection to its language but discarded it, killed it by the most heinous operations imaginable. This living language was killed by a highly metallic silence that worked incessantly like some super-efficient lawn-mower until an impenetrable speechlessness came into existence.

As the remnants of my dead ideals continued to flood me, I picked up my old rain coat and ventured out into the rain to be suffused by the melancholy flowing outside. The solitude in the flat seemed like a death sentence. My wife had taken our two children along with her after a quarrel. I had beaten the shit out of her. I kicked and punched her in the stomach even though she was four months pregnant. I had problems. It had become established that I was an inveterate wife-beater. There was a rippling pool of rain-water in front of the building. The security bulbs were dead and darkness swelled everywhere. I walked down the water-logged street avoiding the puddles when I could. Then I climbed the pedestrian bridge to get to the other side. As I looked down the bridge, the cars below looked like metallic insects pursuing unbending goals with their mainly yellow flashlights.

Things I had once thought about continued to return to me. Wasn't it amazing that there could be some heinous mechanism that could be deployed to institute a reign of total silence? Only that this silence was personal, my sole burden to carry until I had reached the end by the endless smoking of cigarettes. In that pitiless ambience I was to hold onto a relic that could neither comfort nor harm me. I was to be the repository of speechlessness because disgusted by the debaucheries of my lyricism I had passively participated in the killing of a language's music. I had shed occasional tears into the surrounding dryness and my remorse was bloodless, shorn of self-pity through no doing of mine. I was just an inconsequential shard in the most remote futurity of a battlefield which was neither here nor there, since no act of mine or anyone else's could transform my condition into one of ceaseless movement and grace. No excuse could be found to be blood, sperm and real tears again through an exactitude that was without antecedents, that wasn't a correlative of an already lingering presence. And this artificiality was natural because it couldn't call to itself any false authorities. Otherwise, I was to be translated into the confines of an act, within well-defined parameters that have undergone complete fossilisation and therein all progressions were towards a zero. Progressions that couldn't really be so in the most exact sense since an act announced its own death and finality. What was left to be pondered was the rigid aftermath of its own closure, its lack of space and incapacities for regeneration. So it was one and the same thing. It was a state of affairs that described an economy that had lost its power for the definition of other presences. So we ponder the lack of time and mourn a substantiation whose absence was a foregone conclusion.

Thoughts that had long become sterile within me continued to emerge from the barrenness of nostalgia. My tears poured into the rain and glistened under the glare of flashlights. The cars glided down the causeway like little high-tech caterpillars after a prey. Their lights shone with a focused impersonality and rain-water slid down their flanks. The tears continued to fall.

One of my greatest problems has been my inability to hold onto a single end of the pendulum, to follow to consummation the trajectory of a single argument and like a spasm, I kept swimming over diverse moods until I lost the discipline of standing still and moulding into being artifacts meant for the recesses of time. It wouldn't have mattered if they disintegrated into infinity. Neither would it have mattered if I became a victim of my self-induced *sang-froid*. The chill I bore would be the very basis for my actions. In a tweed jacket, a well worn shirt and undone tie, I had resolved to preside over the unfolding silence of my existence. There was to be nothing heroic about my isolation or spiritual devastation. There was to be nothing overtly pathetic either. It was nothing more than a statement, one that had been inscribed upon an immobile horizon with the patience of a true sculptor's hands. Contentment reigned with supreme eloquence along an ineffably melancholic path of a near infinite hiss… I was aware that I had chosen this fate with a volition that was devoid of self-consciousness without ceremony. I had translated myself without much ado into a sign of stableness and in the process I came to lose part of my original ambitions. In short, I became the very antithesis of what I had previously sworn not to become again – a question mark without antecedents and progenies in a certain setting, one that had been totally self-created, of course. I also resolved to contest the numerous meanings that had come to be attributed to me. True, I wanted to become everything in one breath. It was in this same breath that I created my innumerable games which I forgot as soon as they found form and which freed me from the bothersome necessity of analysis. In this condition I had the qualities of Rastafarian hair, cascades of protestations, always affirming and declaiming. So I guess my condition was somewhat akin to Rastafarian hair that had passed through a mill of reggae, punk, hippie rock, hip-hop and hard-core social activism.

The limp and broken old ideals hung in the rain-chilled air like incomplete mementos and smelled like half-deaths. I would never imagine they would have come this far with me. I felt like the fast aging man I was who had known the power of thought and language before being married to indolence and silence. Sometimes, I also felt like an old pugilist who was painfully rediscovering the power of the punch.

The drizzle continued and the flashlights persistently uncovered the thickly whirling melancholy of the night. My wife had gone. Moreover, she had gone with my kids. My life, shattered in pulps. If it hadn't become a lost cause, why would I have condescended to marry such a whore in the first place? I had attempted to build some sort of life with a slut that had absolutely no respect for me even though she was nothing herself. I was a sorry mess but I hadn't the courage to face somebody who could tell me so. Over the last ten or so years, I had been withdrawing into my ever shrinking cosmos feeling there was nothing vital I had to offer. As a young man many people had found me to be quite intelligent and promising. But now as I sunk deeper into the dusk of my life, it became apparent that I had been propelled by surface glitter. The pain of this terrible knowledge had silenced all my vital aspirations. The recalcitrant nitwit I chose for a wife instead of being grateful had constituted herself effectively into my final misery. I had thought that because I could provide her with clothes, three square meals a day and all the other basic comforts, she would remain peaceable. I had thrown parties for her and her whorish friends. I had also spent vast amounts on her extended family. I felt powerless to change anything. Tales of the relative richness of my past lives flitted to her fuelling her greed and wrong-headed ambitions. She wanted more of everything, cars, a much more luxurious home and more fucking children! Being almost thirty years younger than me, this was perhaps understandable. But why did she agree to marry a man who was awaiting the closure of his night? When she spoke, her voice was like a barbarian's spluttering through a broken machine. Yet I withstood her. I bore her insults and base insensitivities with a perseverance that was almost beyond me. I was always hoping she'd change, acquire some level of culture but I've come to realise it is a lost cause. I slowly approached my grave bearing the sharpest burden of my pain. Oh this counterfeit of a bitch! The shame I must bear on her account and which my powerlessness is unable to change. I remember the day I took her to a party given by a friend who was running for a gubernatorial post. In a bid to please me and the friends who sat at our table she started to hoard several bottles of wine. My embarrassed friends started to leave one by one. I mean there was enough for everyone to drink and yet she went on to display her greed and obscene lack of culture before such genteel company. Of course I couldn't reprimand her because she would have taken offence and hen-pecked me out of existence. And the horrid ways she sets the table! Throwing knives and forks everywhere as if a demon was hot at her bum. She could never do things orderly, there had to be a measure of violence even when she granted me a glass of water.

You never leave enough money for anything, she snaps.

But I gave you a cheque only yesterday.

You should come to the market with me to see how prices are skyrocketing!

You always say that.

And you never come!

Having had enough of the rain and its sadness I began my slow march home. By now the streets were truly flooded and the cars were more cautious about how fast they glided. The last thing anyone could wish for was an accident on a rainy night. The legs of my trousers had been soaked up to my knees.

The solitariness of the streets stuck out like a bad dream. I felt a taste of bitterness weighing down on my tongue.

A wide pool had gathered in front of the building and I skirted around it as best as I could. The landing was usually deserted and the silence rang out like a dirge. The air in my flat was as heavy as a room full of mourners. Tani hadn't come back. Where could she have gone? I thought. I decided it was best to give her a night before I commenced a search for her. In the refrigerator, was a half-eaten loaf of bread, which I ate with some water. Moments later the electricity went off and the dark night became doubly oppressive. The cockroaches began to emerge from their cracks, invading the kitchen dust-bin which hadn't been emptied for God knew how long. It was too late to attempt to stumble upon an order that a nearly fractured mind had lost the will to contemplate. Too late as well to prepare to make the most of a night that had gone terribly sour. Then it dawned on me that the rain wasn't a nuisance after all. A coolness issued forth and disarmed what might have been a hot frustrating night as the electricity had been put out. I undressed and lay on my bed waiting for sleep to come. It didn't. The emptiness of the flat turned out to be nightmarish. Tani's revolt tore through me like a loud wail. Why had I become encumbered by an exhaustion that was beyond my endurance? Could it be some folly lost in the middle of my tribe? A century or so ago, my tribe had been made up of predominantly farmers. They tended the farmsteads that were located at the edges of the village. Yams, cocoyams and beans formed part of the communal diet. The monkeys swung from tree to tree and at nights, leopards sometimes came to infringe on the innocence of the sleeping village carrying off a goat or so. Hyenas did the same. The white man had established his kind of order and mode of worship. The innocence of those times came under the watchful as well as destructive hammer of another civilisation and continued to bristle among the undergrowths. Bill Large, who was a miner, planted his seed in scores of women and his upsprings continued to live within the spirit of our tribe. Large had come looking for all kinds of minerals: cobalt, gold, diamonds, vanadium, platinum, chromite, manganese, phosphate, antimony, copper, uranium, iron ore, lead, zinc, columbium and potash. It was said that Olubun, my great-great-grandfather who was a prominent hunter had enough talismans to put a whole tribe of lions to sleep. He wore leopard pelt as his hunting gear and could disappear at will. But these acts of disappearance could be dangerous, as it was said that he sometimes found himself flung into the depths of oceans, the tops of trees and the peaks of mountains. He ate elephants and lions so his bones hardened where those of other men paled with softness from eating too many common types of food. Old age took him to his grave and then the village came to realise it had lost an irretrievable toughness. Olubun's departed spirit could only hang limply as a breath of death upon the canvas of life. His spirit also felt like an old man's voice flailing at the edges of a pale and sickly hamlet.

Then a tribe of warriors approached the village from the drylands. They came with spears, guns and horses. Their king rode wearing an extensive gown of resplendent whiteness. Around his equally white headgear was a blood red sash, as we were told. The blood of our men flowed towards the outer reaches of the village chased by the inconsolable screaming and weeping of the women. The old men and boys were taken away to work on the farms of the victors. The few white men who remained continued to spread the word of the Lord amongst women whose grief hadn't stopped them from listening. Every two years or so, the victors repeated their raids, rapes and pillage. The word of the Lord continued to be administered like some cancerous growth amidst a people whose sorrows had greatly softened the collective heart.

Some of the survivors of the raids reasoned -urged on by the white man's brain- that it would be better if they took to the surrounding hills. Old Oroke was located in a valley and their enemies encountered virtually no problems in descending on them.

Life on top of the hills was much better than living in the depths of the valley except that the weather on the heights wavered between extremes. The women continued to do the farm work while the men mourned the decimation of their brethren. A strange cowardly affliction began to eat into them until they even refused to come downhill. The women feared the worst had happened but continued to exhort their children to venture to the lowlands and acquire the secrets of strength from there. Their children came home and when they behaved arrogantly, they were killed by their mothers through magical means for ritual purposes. Oroke continued to experience the corrupted cycle of misery, death and defeat brought on by its own hands rather than foreign ones. Every man from the village went out for the struggle of life only to be brought back dead (and usually in his prime) for his burial. An old man who grew to taste the sadness of his night had said, "Our tongue is the poison that consumes our children".

At sundown, the men drank palm wine beneath mango trees while they waited to visit their mistresses in the homes of husbands who were in most cases obliging. The mistresses would have prepared their families' meal and then retired to fuck their boyfriends in their quarters while the children played and sang songs under the moonlight. The men who were mainly gossips avoided all plans for war and concentrated on fucking each other's wives. The women continued with their ceaseless toil with a dignity that was at times interspaced with madness and rumours of witchcraft. An old woman would sometimes break into the marketplace totally naked to recount past evils. The men sang their sacrilegious songs at village ceremonies and used the proceeds they received from singing their songs to buy more wine. By the time they woke up from their slumber, other peoples of the world had gone far into the future. "What was there to be seen in the future? They teased, "Every stray dog eventually finds its way home and I'll tell you what, a piece of real arse is better than one in a looking-glass". They laughed. When the time of modern day politics came, they found out, although a bit too late, that a dog was better prowling over strange lands. Indeed there is a strength in strangeness because it is rare. And now it was almost too late to compete with other dogs who had learned all the secret paths of hidden lands. The men from Oroke who discovered the secrets did so at a great price-- their lives. Those who remained at home invariably fell for wine, women and cheap talk. And the one or two in a generation who clung to some real courage paraded the byways of the village like discarded, isolated branches that refused to die. One such man who was a relation of my mother had told my father: "I am not ready to restrict myself to some frigging hut so I look for witches at night acting out their obscenities. And what does that slut of mine do? She goes about doing you know what. And what have I done, I too locked up her bloody cunt with a padlock and need I say every man who goes there is merely wasting his time". He said this roaring with laughter!

A period came when cowardice completely emasculated the spirit of Oroke. The men lost the last vestiges of pride and the women started to behave like troglodytes, emerging naked from the hills to fetch firewood or water from the streams below. The government made their plight a national issue and foreign journalists from Germany, the United States, and Switzerland went into the inaccessible hills to record what they could. Hunger ravaged the villagers because they were afraid to go to their farmlands, which cattle rearing nomads had taken over. Their medicinemen were made scapegoats of their fear and misfortunes. Those that weren't killed were chased to the outskirts of the land where most of them became insane. Those who retained some semblance of sanity continued to utter incantations to lethal plants and roots. These were plants and roots that contained the secrets of life and strength. When things finally got better, everyone had forgotten the legends of conquests that had shored up their spirit. For every man that tasted the bud of success, scores laid in the ground eaten by the collapse of the heart.

I, who had been to many lands of great strength, had finally returned to our cycle of defeat. I had married into our hollowness when I should have been enjoying the results of my numerous adventures. Such were the thoughts that disturbed me through the long night. At dawn when I got up to make myself a cup of tea, I smelt urine issuing from the carpet. I was sure my eight-year-old son had done it and my wife hadn't bothered to clean it up. I got a bowl of water and some detergent and scrubbed off the offensive odour. As the day wore on, panic got the better of me. My wife hadn't come back. I was virtually useless in the kitchen and hunger had begun to take its toll on me. What a bloody coward I was! My wife gives me any shit to eat and I'm only too grateful.

What had I gotten myself into? The bastard! He's ruined me. Oh my baby, I've miscarried! And to think how long it took to conceive this child. And the fucking bastard murdered it! He killed it because he has children all over town. God would never forgive him. Just because he's got numerous children he hasn't bothered to claim doesn't give him the right to kill my *own* baby.

Don't get more upset than you already are.

Upset? I'm fucking outraged! Do you know what I had to go through to get pregnant in the first place, Shadun?

I know, Tani, please just be silent.

No, I can't remain silent, he calls me uncultured, illiterate and whatnot, but even the men back in the village are not as barbarous as he is. I should have married a much younger and enlightened guy instead of that old bag of bones. He virtually deceived me, pretending he had so much money, he didn't know how to spend it. There was a young Ph.D holder who really desired to marry me and I kept him off only to allow that evil man to be my ruin. Oh stomach!

Tani, why don't you come and lie down - you'll start bleeding again.

I can't bleed anymore than this. I even want to die now. What's the use? He said he went to school and yet there is nothing he knows. His business is in ruins. He can't even run a small outfit decently with all his illustrious qualifications. He's a total disgrace, a half-man. Where would he be if it wasn't for me? There's nothing he does for me. Left to him he'd rather sit brooding waiting for death to come and take him. I brought him hope and he wants to kill me for it. Do you know how much I've spent trying to have this baby?

I know.

I've been to all sorts of native doctors, drinking and swallowing potions and concoctions of all sorts. I have run naked at night appeasing the witches. I have placed offerings to the gods and goddesses of fertility so that I can conceive. I would ask him to join me in the rituals and he'd mock them. Sometimes he even got angry and threatened to eject me from his house. A house that is more like a disgrace! The chairs are all torn and filthy and yet he does nothing about it! He uses a gramophone in this day and age and he calls himself an educated modern man. The television shows very blurred pictures and yet he refuses to have it fixed properly. I guess what he regards as modernity does not extend beyond eating biscuits and downing endless cups of tea. All the girls I started off with all drive posh cars and create havoc at the markets with their spending sprees. I have to penny pinch all the time in town. Is that what life is about? I mean how long does one have in this life anyway to allow some old bastard whose time has come to put the lid over one? But I tell you, I shan't let him kill me. I know he's just looking for someone to kill, someone who would slave away for him. In me, he's got more than he bargained for. I'm ready for him and I'll teach him the lesson of his life. The bastard. But why did my life have to turn out like this? Isn't God supposed to guard and protect His children?

Tani, don't wear yourself out please.

I'm already worn out! I'm not going back to that house! I'm going to show him I can survive without him. The foolish bastard.

After two weeks, Tani went back to stay with her husband, Solomon Wenku. Wenku had had to pay a heavy price to lure her back. He went about asking her friends where she could be found. Many who knew avoided telling him. Eventually he found out she was staying with Shadun, who was a trader. Shadun was slightly older than Tani and because the latter had married a much more successful man, the former was never encouraged to play a prominent role in the relationship. Shadun was the one who had to run around doing monkey work. She went to markets to buy all sorts of things for Tani. If Tani was having an affair she covered up for her. When Tani came to stay with her, she was forced to play the role of matchmaker between two difficult partners. She seemed to have reconciled herself to the fact that hers was just a secondary existence as far as Tani was concerned. It was never uttered, but was always explicit rather than implied.

Solomon was appalled by Shadun's dwellings. He never believed a wife he married would agree to live in that sort of place after staying with him for a number of years. The house stood right at the edge of a long gutter which ran beside a decrepit side street. A squalid bypath. Little boys were playing football on the jagged surfaces of the path on barefoot. Broken bottles and garbage were strewn everywhere. In the neighbourhood, many houses were erected from cardboard, plywood and corrugated roofing sheets. The gutters' slimy muck had spilled over and had made haphazard black maps on the red dust. There were many illegally connected electric cables criss-crossing the gnarled electric poles. Well-worn tatters of kites hung from the cables that had caught them. The kites looked like dead birds that had frozen in their petrifaction. Nonetheless, lively warm breezes continued to breathe life into the deadness of the tattered wings. A pretty young woman stops and she's accorded a guard of honour by a broken ragged formation of young boys. She's very aware of her body but it is obvious that the awareness goes no further. The boys resume their game, shouting along the path. Later on, they grow tired of football and begin to strike themselves with whips made of cardboard. Their clear shrill voices rang in the air. The adults who are watching them call the cowardly ones among them bastards.

Solomon was admitted into a dingy sitting place that hadn't enough room for more than four men. The stench in the room had been stopped dead in its tracks and then had been resurrected many times over by fresh farts, sweat and piss so one could describe it as nondescript. Tani was not present in the room and neither were the children. Solomon sat making conversation with Shadun's husband, who was a bricklayer. He felt sorry for himself for what he had gotten himself into. The man, Bundu had several tribal marks across his cheeks and he was obviously pleased to have such an important visitor. He sent for drinks to be brought in by his own children. They had stood by the doorway with their bumpy tonsured heads in rags looking at the august visitor with hungry eyes. A strong smell of urine had swept across Solomon's face.

How's business, sir?

Oh well, we do our best.

It's the same here, activity in the construction industry has virtually halted and the few construction jobs around are being contracted to foreign firms.

Solomon looked more carefully into his face and he didn't seem so foolish after all. Bundu on his part realised the impact of his words and became more confident.

We black men are our own worst enemies, we do nothing than plot the downfall of our own brothers thereby giving our enemies the chance to contribute their own quota to our ruin. Afterall, what do those bloody foreign firms know that I don't? I've been a bricklayer for more than twenty years and I have worthy evidence for my work. Through my work, I married my wife and she bore me eight kids and I feed them through it. I set up my wife as a trader. In my family no one is idle. No one at all. My first son is already learning bricklaying, while the second one is apprenticed to a carpenter. The third girl is training to be a seamstress and three more are street traders. The last two are still too young, but in time they too will become traders like their mother. And I tell you sir, I have found out this is the only way a family like ours can survive these atrocious times. We have become the envy of every other family in the neighbourhood and by the precious grace of God we shall continue to excel.

Solomon, towards the end of the monologue, got bored. He perceived the man was doing a little too much to impress. But what could he do? If he hadn't provoked his wife to the extent that she had had to move out he wouldn't have had to go through this rigmarole. Some lukewarm beer bottles were brought out and placed clumsily on the centre table by the bricklayer's children. They had also invited the other children who lived in the other tenements within the dwelling. The young boys stood at the entrance grinning at Solomon and hoping that he would throw them a few coins.

Shoo, get out you rats! Don't your bloody parents give you any bones to eat? Dogs! said Bundu. The boys ran out onto the little street to resume their games. Solomon wondered how people who existed within the lowest depths of squalor could remain so unselfconscious. Poverty never seemed to bother to contemplate itself. It never seemed to worry how medical bills would be paid in the event of injury and disease. It never lost its sense of humour for long especially in the eyes of children.

My kids don't behave that way. Such mindless monkeys. I hate this neighbourhood. I hope to leave soon.

Solomon knew he was merely boasting. Things had gotten so bad that getting the smallest and most horrid room would cost a fortune. The only place he could go was into the streets like so many other homeless families whose dead dreams were lost in the ordeals that visited the helpless.

Where is my wife? He asked finally.

Oh, you know women. She feels very highly offended sir… If I were you I'd take it slow on her. Sir, there's still plenty of time to get round to that.

Time? I want her back as soon as possible. After all, I've paid for her bride price.

Oh, very well, sir but…

Look, no buts, where is she?

Call your mother for me. He said to one of his children.

Shadun came in and knelt down in greeting. Solomon could barely reciprocate.

Welcome sir, it's an honour to have you here.

Good to see you.

No one knew exactly how to broach the main issue. Anyway, such issues were usually skirted round first.

Your wife is well, she said finally.

Oh.

She doesn't believe you love her anymore…She's had a miscarriage.

Bad luck. Solomon said with unhidden cruelty.

She's certain you don't want her back.

She must be kidding!

Well, you'll have to prove otherwise.

How?

You have to bring a sort of small bride price…Two bales of *ankara* material, white brocade, two big chickens, one bottle of wine and a bottle of gin. A sack of rice and one sack of beans.

Good heavens! This is daylight robbery. I'm paying her bride price all over again!

Well, those are the things you must bring if you want her back.

Solomon stood up to go. Outside, the massed clouds had a wateriness over them. In the courtyard in front, a large number of kids were having a late lunch of rice and palm oil. A little boy of about two particularly stood out. He had ugly mosquito bites all over his face and already a long scar marked his large forehead. He held onto a greasy plastic bowl of rice and plastic spoon, which he was also throwing about in the dirt. When he observed that his mother, who was seated on a small stool had a little piece of bread, he flung his spoon away again and dashed to her. Playfully his mother refused to give him any bread and then he threw a loud tantrum. Still she didn't offer him some so he grabbed wildly and took it away from her. Satisfied, he went to pick up his spoon that lay in the dirt and continued to strut about the yard with his greasy bowl of rice.

The electricity still hadn't been restored. The entire flat smelt of rotten fish. In the kitchen, stagnant pools of water from the temporarily dead refrigerator formed on the floor. Solomon opened the refrigerator to let out the stale air. Instead of an integrated coolness, a dead warmth hung mid-air like a bad omen. The pawpaw was rotten, the oranges were soggy, the stew stale. Almost everything had gone bad. He took out the large batch of wilted vegetables and deposited them in the bin. Hunger loomed large but the rot was more overwhelming. The entire flat seemed to be collapsing in a macabre fashion. It was as if monolithic graves were springing out and freezing in the midst of the rot. Perhaps, when all is said and done, rats would inherit the earth.

The following day, being not exactly able to bear the oppressiveness, Solomon ventured out to purchase the items he had been asked to. Towards sunset he went again to the slum where Bundu and his family lived. No little boys were playing football on the cracked uneven street but the dead kites still hung like dead doves on the numerous illegal electric lines. The sun shone as if recovering from a bad hangover after a torrential downpour. But the art of survival hadn't shed its incense of innocence and rejuvenation. The corruption waxed so thickly in the hovels that patches of life clung together like torture chambers.

Shadun was nowhere to be found but Bundu was at home. This time he was to act as the go-between. Solomon was very much against making his private affairs anyone's business. Bundu was already using the opportunity to get more friendly than was necessary, dropping uncalled for hints about how a man was to manage his family, most especially his wife. Bundu barely acknowledged the goods Solomon had brought. His children were much more excited.

Let's go for a drink if you don't mind.

They went to an open place beneath a cluster of mango trees. Darkness had started to swirl like a serpent. Many drinkers were gathered swilling down endless bottles of beer and eating greasy peppered chicken and snails. An unruly pack of young homeless boys were playing music with empty tins that they used as drums. In the midst of the din they created for the enjoyment of the drinkers, they asked for alms.

Bundu and Solomon found a long bench to sit on. Soon they were served two warm bottles of beer. The drumming continued frantically and the mosquitoes gathered in masses below their knees.

Take it easy on your wife now.

Solomon couldn't endure the pontification, especially from someone who was his social inferior. He had to listen to a bricklayer who lived in the worst of slums claiming to know better than him in simple matters of organisation. It was so annoying. But there was no denying the fact that he wanted his wife back. He was sick and tired of eating stale bread and tea. He was sick of having to endure the smell of the putrid bin in the kitchen, the dust in the ghostly living room, the air that had become heavy from lack of human company. He was also sick of having no options in bed.

You must be ready to accept that women are devils but they are necessary evils. They finished their bottles of beer and ordered more. The beer bottles were warm as usual because there wasn't any electricity. The atmosphere was flat with heat. The drumming persisted and broke only when the money that had been collected was to be shared.

Expect your wife tomorrow night.

That was all Solomon had waited to hear. He hated the suspense the man had put him through. He looked at Bundu again. He was a thin man of average height who had married a woman who turned to a skilful but extremely unassuming social climber. Her friends were much higher than her on the social scale so she dealt with them with a natural meekness she only lost when she was with her husband at home. Her tastes had outstripped his in value and sophistication and there was nothing he could do to catch up. He regarded her rise with mixed feelings. First of all, he knew she was bound to be having affairs with men who could finance her tastes and this made him sad and uneasy. On the other hand, he was glad to be married to probably the most glamorous woman in the neighbourhood. The hand-outs she brought home from her well-to-do friends were the envy of all. A little down the street, she kept a stall where she sold imported fabrics. Most of the other women were mainly gossips or traded in foodstuffs and vegetables. Shadun never went out of her way to show that she was superior but the difference was there for all to see. Bundu continued to drink, caught within a welter of contrasting feelings. But he was glad he had finally made Solomon's acquaintance. He was sure he had made some impression on him and by virtue of that, he could go and see him whenever he wanted.

****

Tani moved back into the flat fuming. It seemed as if she were coming back against her will. Nothing could be further from the truth. Those nights lying cramped within a living room right in the middle of a slum had taught her to appreciate the numerous comforts her home provided.

It's like a pig sty in here, God!

She opened the windows and continued to fume. Solomon was thinking she had cooked some food for dinner, but she hadn't. The dark night wore into depths of ennui. Their two children were happy to be back at home once more and went into their bedroom to play and then sleep. They, too, had nothing to eat that night.

Tani flung her clothes, including her underwear, on the armchair in their bedroom. She was always doing that, never bothered to hang them up. Solomon moved like a ghost onto the bed while she continued to make distracting noises. Each of her movements seemed to speak, seemed to be a pointed protest. Beneath her breath were barely subdued hisses. When she finally came to the bed with only a wrapper around her large-boned body, an excruciating wall of silence stood shrieking between them. Solomon was unable to find sleep throughout the night. Tani tossed all through and hissed at intervals.

Dawn came into the room with the uncertainty of a drunk. The electricity hadn't been restored. The room seemed overburdened by both natural and artificial darknesses. Tani stood up to prepare the family's breakfast. A pleasure warmed Solomon's intestines.

Breakfast was laid. Fried eggs with a lot of vegetable oil, slices of bread and tea. Tani sat drinking noisily from a mug of tea while her husband ate with obvious relish.

The rains aren't too good this year, she said.

Oh?

Everything is so bloody expensive.

Yeah?

A basket of tomatoes costs the head of a human being.

Really?

A gallon of adulterated cooking oil would fetch a pair of testicles.

So?

The cost of a bag of rice would buy a nation.

You don't say.

A bag of beans cannot be bought!

Are we to stop eating?

That's what it's coming to and the next thing would be death.

You need a fortune to get enough vegetables for a pot of soup to feed a small family like ours.

Incredible!

The quality of fertiliser is getting worse.

Mere poisons, I think.

Chicken has been priced out of most homes.

I noticed.

Soon we shan't be able to afford tomatoes for our soup.

God forbid.

The cost of living has reached the point of death.

God save us!

After breakfast, feeling a little at peace with himself, Solomon ventured out to the gate under a weak sun. The enormous dust bin outside the compound immediately dampened his spirits. It had become overloaded with refuse of all kinds: rotten oranges, numerous cellophane bags that stank of stale food, rancid rice, dead rats that had been killed elsewhere and fruit peelings of all sorts. On the ground around it lay more refuse and rotten leaves. A rat suffering from an acute skin disease ran through a trail of muck. A car rode past and splashed water into the garbage. Just as he was about to turn back in, a man, in black oily clothes came and started rummaging in the bin. It wasn't clear at first that he was mentally ill because so many men had taken to making their living from waste products. It was when he started to eat the rotten remains of melon soup wrapped in a transparent cellophane bag did it occur to Solomon that all wasn't well with him. Solomon cast one more pitiful glance at him and then faced the door. Tani was washing the dishes with the assistance of Lokoma, her first daughter who she didn't like very much. She preferred her son, Sukuma, a boy of about eight who had very little in his head. Lokoma's birth had given Tani a lot of pain and hardship and somehow she hadn't forgotten about it and the bitterness had tainted irreparably her relationship with the girl.

Would you go and fetch me some more water, you pig! You have to be told everything, idiot!

Sukuman laid on the couch in the living room playing with a broken toy gun. When Solomon appeared he jumped up and ran up to his father. Solomon always showered affection on the boy, but it wasn't clear whether he really loved him. The boy was so stupid, but he was unable to admit to himself that he had fathered such a dullard. With Lokoma, the situation was more unequivocal. He didn't believe he was her father and behaved as such. Tani on her part never went ahead to challenge him for it. All she complained of was his cold attitude towards her, which was bound to affect the relationship between the two children.

Tani always washed the dishes and cleaned up the flat with a barely hidden violence. She seemed to want it inscribed loud and clear that she was in charge, that she was around, as it were. She threw cutlery in drawers so harshly that they began to give way. She had broken so many plates from her vigorous way of tossing them around. When she worked, caustic religious songs that proclaimed victory over her enemies were her favourites.

A friend from Solomon's past life came on a visit. She was a medical doctor who had helped him in the past and her father had been his friend whilst he had been alive. Tani eyed her with coarse suspicion at first and then very listlessly asked Lokoma to call Solomon from the bedroom. She continued to sing her religious songs of victory with her high pitched, untrained voice. Of course the bewildered visitor calmly ignored her. Solomon hugged his old friend and gave her a kiss. That didn't go down well with Tani, who was now thinking there was more to their relationship. She sang her songs even louder, but no one took any notice of her.

Lizzy, so nice… You know.

Yeah.

I haven't seen you since the death of your father.

That's right and I was pondering what must have gone wrong.

Oh, nothing, except that I have a new wife.

Oh, you do?

Tani, please come and meet Lizzy.

Tani looked up from the chest of drawers she was wiping with a rag and said a word of greeting as if reluctantly.

Lizzy is a gynaecologist.

Oh how nice, then she can help me!

But you don't have any problems.

You never know. I may need her.

Come and meet her then.

Ha do do?

Fine, thank you and you?

Fine tanke you.

Tani immediately observed that the other woman had a much more refined personality than hers and was therefore a threat to her. Her countenance changed and she quickly excused herself to resume her cleaning. Lizzy sensed she wasn't quite welcome, so she cut short her conversation with Solomon and took her leave. Tani didn't bother to see her to the door.

She wanted a child. More children. But she was not willing to cede her place in the home to an impostor. Secondly, sometimes western medicine may not be the best for a condition that may involve supernatural circumstances.

After lunch, she went to see her friend Shadun again.

I think there is an external hand in my affair…I want it out!

What do you mean?

Can't you read the signs? After passing through the eye of a needle to have a child, I lost it just like that.

But it was your husband's fault.

Don't be a fool! Some evil forces were just using him. He was the medium they used to accomplish their wicked deed.

In that case we shall have to go and see Baba.

Yes, we have to.

Let's make it two days time.

Solomon sat at home listening to the babbling of his idiotic son. He was the only company he could get readily since his gradual withdrawal from the world. He knew he was lucky to be able to have three square meals a day while a huge silent majority sat dying out in droves from hunger, disease, heat and neglect. His pension and savings were meagre and if he had decided not to marry again they might perhaps have lasted him until his last days. But it was now certain that his finances would be exhausted because of the spendthrift he had for a wife. Every business venture he had set up for her had flopped. She didn't seem to possess the basic discipline necessary for managing even the smallest business. She would start off with a lot of gusto that ran out as soon as she felt there wasn't enough money coming in. It never occurred to her to give the venture a year or two to grow. She would muddle up the accounts and become bored in due course. The business would sink and she would merely shrug her shoulders and get ready to move on. Solomon would shake his head. Soon she would be gripped by the paroxysm of a new business idea, which she would begin to nag Solomon to finance.

This one can't fail-- it will make me rich and I shall be free of your financial tyranny!

I haven't got any more to sink into any business.

You see, just as I had thought! You never have any money to finance anything that isn't of interest to you. Wicked man!

Let me just tell you that I'm not prepared to spend the remaining years of my life with a good-for-nothing old man who can't see beyond his nose. Don't you know what everyone is saying and doing outside? How could you when all you do is sit on your arse from sun up to sun down. If you don't finance it, I will get money from friends and that would embarrass you.

Solomon could never win with her. She seemed to have the impression that he had so much money she could play with. She had married him for money. He did his best to make her comfortable, but it was never enough. To worsen matters, her mouth stank! She didn't even know how to give a kiss anyway. What nerve! He had picked up an uncivilised village girl to spend the rest of his days with him and it had turned out all wrong. He hadn't the strength or courage to change anything now. He had fallen for the Rousseausian lure for nature and natural things untouched by the casuistry of civilisation. He had thought he could tame and domesticate her in a way that would be beneficial to her as well. He remembered the time he was courting her at Oroke when she was a girl of twenty or so. He remembered how she knelt down before him even when she wanted to give him a glass of water. She couldn't even look into his eyes. Now she had become a tigress in his home and he an old lion that had lost its roar, its will to dominate. He had wanted her to remain in the village so that when he left the city for some rustic serenity, she would be there to minister to his needs. But she too had heard numerous tales about the city and the wealth to be made and enjoyed there.

Darling, you're looking so ill and lean, why don't you let me come and live in the city with you?

Oh, never mind I'll be alright.

After a number of similar visits, Solomon gave way to her pleas. He also thought it wouldn't be such a bad idea to have his children going to school in a metropolis where they were certain to learn more. She came with her bag of troubles and transformed herself into a serpent beyond control. In her eyes, a beauty queen is what she had turned into with her bleached skin. She became a sort of ogre because everything she touched captured her odour. The glasses, the cutlery, the meals she prepared, everything bore the indelible mark of her scent. And then she forgot her history, forgot that she had been a simple village girl who could only have achieved some success in life through whoring. She wasn't cut out for any kind of formal training. The best trade she could have learnt was tailoring or something similar. How had he met her if it wasn't through some form of whoring whether implicit or explicit? She had emerged third in the village beauty contest and everyone called her the "giraffe". He had been the chairman of the occasion and naturally all the contestants wanted to meet him. Tani had been the most aggressive of them all. She was said to have sworn to kill any girl who had stood in her way now that she had lost the main prize. As a young girl, Tani was reputed to be friendly with all the prominent medicine men in the villages around. If she wanted a man, she got him and Solomon had not been an exception.

Solomon remembered the night of the beauty contest and a sad smile almost parted his lips. As chairman of the event, the band in charge never wearied of calling his name!

Solo goes solo
Solo does it alone
Though a great lover is Solo

He had parted with all the money in his pockets, but of course everyone thought he had more and that was why the contestants wanted to meet him.

After the event, anytime he was in the village, Tani would visit him with a couple of her friends. They were always hoping he would give them large sums of money when they were leaving, but he never did. Instead, he would offer them a bottle of wine, which was a real luxury in those hazy days. Tani was always fighting to direct the conversations and her friends had to give in to her. One thing led to another until he was confronted with being responsible for her pregnancy. It wasn't any good dragging that kind of case in the provinces, as young boys fathered children without much fuss and for a man of his age and standing to deny what everyone had been suspecting would be going beyond the pale.

Solomon remembered where Tani had stayed with the children the last time they had quarrelled. She wasn't any better than the slum. She could have gone on living there without much thought because she had no background whatsoever. All her claims to status and a good social standing were based on the pipe-dreams she once had and the dreams she saw for the future. She held onto Solomon like a torch for that future but saw the light flickering weakly like a lantern in a tempestuous gale. She was prepared to shake him like a dead root until she was able to will her dreams, the dreams nourished by her hunger, into fruition. She was willing to kick her way into the day of the mermaids where all hungers, her own overwhelming hunger, will be drowned. Solomon disgusted her because he wasn't hungry or imaginative enough to share in her dreams. He had silently joined the ranks of the vegetative where every spluttering gesture is filled with death and silence. He was drawing her down into those ranks of death but she was resentful and unwilling. Her hunger lusted after the glittering toys of light.

Tani had gotten Solomon like a joke. When he was courting her or rather when they were pursuing each other she was an awfully bad cook. Not that she had improved much since then, but in those days she couldn't even produce a decent plate of burnt eggs. It always had to turn out worse. So she would get her friends who knew how to cook to prepare a meal while she and Solomon had sex. He would lie spent upon the narrow bed while she dashed off to the kitchenette to see how far her friends had gone.

Please make it the best thing you've ever cooked in your lives.

You're such a smart ass, one of her friends would say.

For three years the deception went on and she and her friends joked about Solomon's dimness behind his back. He never suspected anything and ravished his meals like a gluttonous boy oblivious of those who were around. They winked and laughed at him.

Are you enjoying the film?

Very much so, sir.

I must remember to bring you new videotapes when I come back.

Solomon would invite his relatives who hated Tani to his chalet for a meal.

She's such a wonderful cook.

Oh.

Come and see for yourselves.

No one was bold enough to tell him he was dating a whore. Solomon was too generous in giving them drinks and they didn't want to lose that favour. The bravest amongst them sneered casually when Tani was mentioned. Others having had their fill of drinks would shake their heads sadly, snickering at Solomon's choice.

I don't see what he fancies in that village whore.

It's such a shame.

My son's sons were the ones that used to fuck her.

Mine as well.

A great pity.

One night when I was going home after an evening drink and lo and behold what did I see? Parked at the edge of the road on that starless night was a white car. I approached it as carefully as a leopard angling for a kill. It seemed there was some moaning and a bit of arguing going on. I gave the car a big bang with my hand and said come out now or I will kill you both! And who did I see, Dada the motor mechanic clutching Tani. Needless to say both of them were naked and shivering in the cold. I laughed and whistled on into the night.

That can't be true.

Is that so? Then go and ask Dada.

He has a grudge against Tani and Solo. I'm sure he would spill the beans!

I believe him.

So do I.

I'm sure she's had a bath for him if you know what I mean.

That's the only likely thing.

A big pity.

A great shame.

Solomon would leave Tani behind in the village while he went back to the city to continue his life. She was virtually a virgin when I met her, he would think to himself. The only person he knew that had had an affair with her was Laoro, his cousin.

She's a great girl, go on and marry her. His cousin had told him. Laoro was a light-skinned man with a record of criminal activities who wanted a loan from Solomon. And he was prepared to say anything to get it. When he eventually got what he wanted he stopped coming to see Solomon and joined others in calling him Lord of a Whore. He didn't pay back the loan either.

I would never forgive that cousin of mine for being such a fool, he told a group of friends who had gathered to share drinks in a bar one night.

Tani felt the heat the villagers had turned upon her. She knew it was about time she started to plot her exit. But first she had to get him to pay her bride price. Her enemies stood ranged on all sides as if they were attempting to prevent her from entering the home she so much desired.

For one, there was Benu, Solomon's ex-wife to contend with. She was a cantankerous middle aged woman who had three children. Benu was no ordinary woman. Her ways were hellish and so were her means of seeking revenge. Benu never wanted to cede her home to an upstart, an uncivilised money-grabbing whore. She had thought her divorce from Solomon would completely ruin him. She wanted to see the end of him and spit over his grave. The alimony she got from the divorce was more than disappointing. Her lawyers had made her believe that the settlement would plunge Solomon into the deepest pit of penury. They had been wrong to stake their hopes so high in a patriarchal society. Benu's financial standing went from bad to precarious. As the days wore on, curses were what she sent down the wind to Solomon, her life's main heartache.

Such an evil man your father is – bad. Tell him I said so to you. Tell him the blood of all mothers of the earth is against him and he would soon fall. He's the most brazen womaniser I've ever met in my life. He's the greatest curse of my life. I wanted a life of peace and tranquillity but had the misfortune of falling into the hands of a cad. None of my children would take after him. Never! God forbid! I'd rather die than have it happen. The fucking bastard! The sole ambition of his life is to slave away for cunt! That's all he'll ever know and that's why his life is in ruins.

Mummy, it isn't that bad.

Shut up you fool! What do you know? I was the one who anointed your head with blood and you feel you know better than me already. Your father, child, is an evil man. I was married to him long enough to know that. If it wasn't for me he would have left you all to die. My stay in his house was one of great sorrow and pain. I had to battle against all sorts of visible and invisible obstacles. Your father attempted to steal my mind many times, but my head was too strong for him.

She looked around the little flat in which she lived. The furniture was old and broken. The carpeting had been handed down and she couldn't stand the over congestion. She had never believed her life would fall to so low an ebb.

I have slaved all my life to build a home. And look at me now, your father is turning me into a wreck!

The entire flat smelt of kerosene, which she had to use for cooking because she could no longer afford to buy the gas to which she had been accustomed. On most evenings, she went to the neighbourhood church to pray for Solomon's ruin. After all, he was the cause of all her problems.

How can I work to build something only to be alive to watch a whore, Tani or whatever her name is, enjoy the fruit of my labour? God doesn't sleep. He knows I've been a good and faithful wife, so I cannot suffer. This is only temporary. I shall achieve success and Solo would come begging me to take him back and I shall spit on his face then. He had his chance to be a good husband but he lost it. I shall pour hot water on his head.

****

She went to a river one evening as the sun was setting. She wore a deep brown *ankara* blouse and wrapper with snakelike patterns that matched the dirty waters in front of her. There were three empty gourds, representing each of her three children, which she placed on the banks. Rowing far into the river, in canoes, were the sad figures of fishermen who were casting their nets with very little hope. A profusion of hyacinths dotted the sombre waterscape. On the banks were untended cloisters of weed and shells. The clouds loomed in a state of inertia.

God make my children superstars
Let their names ring at the four corners of the earth.
These calabashes here are the symbols of my womb.

Protect them from evil winds and spirits of the world. Let roads open up their mouths in safety for them, let them be the sunshine of my dusk and make my evening free from tears. You know that I have wronged no one and you have seen the wrongs done to me. Make Tani's womb sterile and let her two children grow to be the monsters that they are. Let them be of no use to themselves and their parents. May they all chew the bitterness of their fingers for the reminder of their evil days and let me know the laughter of final night of joy.

Benu finished her prayer, with the indifferent figures of the fisherman rowing on. The vanishing sun cast a reddish glow upon the quiet horizon on the far end. She re-tied her headgear and her wrap, then she floated the three empty gourds on the river's edge to pursue the dreams she had set forth for them. They lingered at first like unsure ducks then they tottered towards the middle. She knelt again to say a few more silent words of prayer and turned to put on her pair of slippers. As she walked away in the other direction, her lone figure didn't turn around to see the three floating gourds. All her hopes congealed within her spare figure, within a solitariness that was carried along with the highest pride.

Vera, who was Benu's last child, needed some money to go back to the boarding school she was attending on the outskirts of town, so she went to see Solomon, her father. She was thirteen years old and not particularly brilliant, but her father loved her for her infantile sense of humour, which appealed to the child in him. Solomon wasn't in. She didn't salute her half-sister and brother as she went right into the master bedroom without knocking. Tani was lying on the bed trying to get some sleep.

Where is my father?

Inside my nose and you can come and fish him out.

Your nose is much too dirty to get into and it's a pity to have a nose that stinks.

What did you just say?

What you just heard.

Get out of here!

This is my father's house, go back to yours.

I said get out of here, you untrained bitch!

You are the greater bitch because you drove my mother out of here.

If your mother weren't a bitch, she would have had the common sense to remain with a man. Now get out!

I'm already leaving. I can't stand your stench.

Tani got terribly inflamed and rose from the bed. She was wearing a pair of shorts and a skimpy T-shirt. She wasn't prepared to let the matter rest like that and proceeded to sweep

Vera out of the flat. Angry words streamed back and forth and Tani was ready to give the rude girl the beating of her life. Vera walked fast out of the house with Tani trailing her closely behind. They got to the front of the building still yelling at each other. The neighbours were attracted to the scene, but no one interfered. It was a show to be merely enjoyed.

Don't ever come back here again, you little scamp.

I will and you can do nothing.

The day you step into this place again you will die!

It's your children who will die.

Your mother dropped you like the piece of shit you are.

And you're the greatest piece of shit.

The crowd that had gathered continued to watch the feud without stepping into it. Many felt Tani was immature to engage a mere girl in such a scandalous exchange of invectives. Vera continued to shout up and down outside the gate, firing off a stream of abuse. Tears of anger strode down Tani's face. She wished she could only lay her hands on her. Vera's mother must be behind this wanton intrusion. Her afternoon had been ruined. Cars passing by slowed down while the drivers and passengers watched and when the crowd had had enough, a few spectators advised Tani to go back inside her apartment. After all Vera was only a child. She backed off gnashing her teeth like a wounded serpent. Solomon would get to hear of this and she would make him act strongly. She slammed the door firmly behind her and shut all the windows. Then she drew the curtains, which made the whole place rather sad and gave it a haunted hue. The children were driven into their bedroom and the portentous silence seemed as oppressive as a hail of bullets. Tani peeped out the window to see if the crowd that had gathered to watch the fracas had dispersed. A few people were still loitering about talking about the violent verbal exchange. In anger she pulled the curtains back into place and hissed. As she waited for Solomon to arrive, her irritation increased. She couldn't find anything to do with herself and she continued to stride the length and breadth of the flat cursing herself for not being able to get her hands on Vera. Still Solomon did not come.

A series of loud violent knocks on the door drove sharp snippets of fear through her. She couldn't imagine who would dare to knock in such an unabashed manner.

Who is it? But she received no answer. The violent knocking continued intermittently, yet she wouldn't open the door. Then a brash voice said:

If you ever dare abuse our mother again you've had it in this city, whore!

It was then Tani knew that Vera's aggrieved brothers had come to pay her a visit. After a while, she became certain they had left, but her fear and anger continued to torment her unabatedly.

The heaviness of the day lingered like a curse. Solomon was driving through a city in ruins and in throes of anguish. Clutters of litter had spilled onto almost every street. Even the potholes were filled with trash. Blackish rainwater clogged with garbage made huge maps on the derelict streets and cracked pavements. Each living breath had a long tale of woe and stench to emit. Along the streets, stranded workers waited in vain for vehicles to take them to their destinations. There was a fuel shortage in town. The few buses that still plied the derelict streets had hiked up their fares immeasurably. A wave of lamentations swept through the despondent throngs that stood at the bus stops waiting for the faintest sign of hope to emerge. Inhabitants of the city who were lucky to have cars that were still running were forced to stop to carry more than their fair share of stranded passengers. Those that refused to help out had their windscreens smashed. On the bridges that hung like incongruous spectres over the dirty infested lagoons, broken armies of seemingly endless people continued the long trek home. Above, in the clouds, were threats of rain. Lines of cars crawled slowly through an eye of hell. Pain and hopelessness had touched everything. Street hawkers continued to run up and down the inflamed, dirt cluttered streets with their wares of pirated cassettes, low quality batteries, fake wrist watches and shoddy dusters hoping to get enough for just another meal. Lying in the middle of the roads were crippled beggars who wallowed in the filth for just a few coins. And then there was another category of beggars who, though healthy, had been crushed under the monstrous weight of unemployment. Some were mothers of twins or quadruplets who had no money to feed their children. They sat on the dirty sidewalks begging those who drove in cars or merely walked by for money. Most of these impoverished mothers were usually gentle about their begging. Perhaps the endless crying of their babies simply wore them out. They just sat drained of hope, breastfeeding their children. Then there were the Arab refugees driven out of their countries by war. The mothers and daughters of this tribe of people were mostly beautiful. But filth had sullied them like gems cast in mud. The mothers and children begged the drivers of crawling vehicles while the fathers sat listlessly in the shade awaiting coins or perhaps a few bites. Things had become really rough for them since beggary started to spread like an infectious disease. At nights, they had to retire to safe places to sleep, otherwise they would be robbed and then beaten by more desperate types. In time, they had come to acquire a class of their own, their style of begging had assumed something of an art form. They went about their task as if it carried along with it a distinction of honour, especially the children, whose cheerfulness and lighted eyes sparkled like the emblems of a chosen race. They refused to work even though most of them looked healthy. Somehow they seemed to bring an inimitable originality to their alms trade.

And then there was yet another breed of beggars who prowled the streets like ferocious hyenas. It was they who brought an aggressive force to begging. They appeared from nowhere and prostrated before their victims calling them by praise-names until they parted with some of their money, which they used in procuring marijuana or stronger hallucinogens. If they could get away with it, they resorted to outright robbery. They too had a distinct appearance that was distorted by a blind ferocity. They walked bent forwards chanting their prayers as if they intended to fall over or launch into an attack. One could never tell what they planned to do. Their lives shifted desperately between the stranglehold of beggary and drug abuse, between the ineffable tragedy of prison life and a hardened criminal's dream of unparalleled success.

Solomon drove on contemplating the infested womb of the city, avoiding high density areas where vice hung like expanses of ponderous clouds from which no one could escape. He whistled tunelessly through the belly of urban catastrophe. The trails of potholes rankled with their own discordant tunes the motor cars couldn't ignore. The vendors of fresh tomatoes and oranges stood like misplaced apparitions behind the almost painful beauty of their wares. A few shops were able to shine with a deceptive kind of opulence, but the surrounding heavy burden of want, decay and squalor gave them a vulgar cast.

Tani was lying on the bed with nothing but a wrap around her body, her buttocks spread out like a fan, her face turned from the door. Solomon came in and found her alluring. His immediate wish was to make love to her. It hadn't even occurred to him that she had prepared nothing for him to eat. On her dark green wrap were patterns of little dragonish fish. The blinds were drawn and the shade flowed within a world of its own. And then her broad backside shifted like a continent. Without a word Solomon pulled gently at her wrap until her heavily bleached body laid exposed. She looked at him and hissed. He had thought that she was sleeping.

I'm hungry.

She didn't say a word and she merely pulled the wrap over herself again without bothering to tie it up because she would have needed to get up. Solomon looked up and down the length of her prostrate body and saw once again the black unbleached spots on her ankles. He repeated his question.

Do you think I would have been alive to continue to make your meals?

He didn't know what to say. All he wanted was something to eat, as she had refused to make love to him. The silence hung pointing at him like a spear, or perhaps a question. Tani decided to break it with a derisive hiss that ran parallel to the previously unbroken shriek of silence.

What the hell is the matter with you, anyway?

Your children came here threatening me with death, and that little daughter of yours, there was nothing on earth she didn't call me.

True?

No it isn't.

Come on.

I can't continue to live my life like an endangered animal.

Tell me what happened.

Just tell them not to come here intending to take my life again.

Well, that's no problem. I'll go and file a report at the police station tomorrow morning.

Solomon started to remove his clothes. The behinds of Tani's thighs were exposed and he could still not resist the urge to have sex with her. She heard him fumbling to get out of his clothes and was thinking that he did his thinking with his balls. For her, it was good thinking because once he put himself in position to act from that point of view, there wasn't much of a problem. She could tie him to agreements that could not have been made without the use of his testicles. He knew this much and he hated himself for that. He hated himself for being a slave to someone whose lovemaking was as basic as a couple of goats scratching their flanks against a tough wall. And he could never teach her the way he would have preferred it because to her it was a game of war in which advantages would be gained and losses incurred. Lovemaking wasn't supposed to be enjoyed. It was immoral to do so. Rather it was an opportunity to show men what babies they were, and how great was their enslavement to their balls. Perhaps the truth of the matter was that Solomon wasn't much more enslaved to the urges of his balls than to Tani's cunt. Nonetheless, the character of her cunt, its forms, features and resilience did a lot to enchant him. He was certain that she wasn't aware of its innate, protean powers. Its varied texture, its range and peculiar elasticity were an irresistible attraction for him. It was true that cunt in general had these myriad characteristics but it was the absolutely unhindered way that Tani's cunt spoke to him directly from itself without her involvement that never ceased to overwhelm him. When they made love, he didn't make love to her as a whole but to her cunt because it was blessed with a highly expressive and versatile language of its own that was solely dependent on itself. The vocabulary of their lovemaking was narrow as was his way of thinking of sex with her. He knew his thinking hadn't moved beyond an adolescent stage and he never really pushed himself to address this shortcoming. As limited as the range of their lovemaking was, it suited him fine because he didn't have to explain anything. All her responses were not only stereotyped, but also very narrow. And try as he may, she too was unwilling to see things differently. They had slept after making love and they seemed like shells on a beach being washed over and shifted by seawater in the endless breakings of waves.

After breakfast the following day, Solomon went to lodge his complaint at the neighbourhood police station. The policemen on duty didn't exactly get his meaning. Here was a man forbidding his own children from coming to see him. The inspector-in-charge thought he was very upset and so was overreacting. He thought he needed to calm down and all will be well again. And so he began to lecture on the need for cohesiveness in family life. Solomon would have none of it and said repeatedly that he wanted to ban his children from coming to his home and that they did so at their own risk.

A young offender was sitting on the bare floor behind the counter without a shirt on. He looked malnourished and was wearing a dirty pair of under-sized white shorts. He got bitten by an insect and stirred violently. A fat, pot-bellied policeman who had a grotesque face and a wet patch around his crotch sitting nearby gave him two slaps as a punishment for jerking. The violent strikes flung the boy across the dusty floor onto an edge of the soiled wooden counter that demarcated the space. In one of the little cells just behind the counter was a naked man held in chains who was lying on the floor. It was clear that he was losing his mind from the way he mumbled to himself and the way he sucked the fingers of one of his hands and scratched his private parts incessantly with the other. He continued to call out with a frail voice, water, water! No one heeded him in the pool of urine in which he laid underneath a swirling coat of flies.

When the inspector-in-charge saw there was no use in convincing Solomon of the folly of what he was about to do, he gave up and registered his complaint. After all he had come in a car and the inspector wasn't ready to incur the wrath of someone who seemed well-to-do. Solomon finally felt appeased and left the stench of urine, degradation and decay behind as he drove off to Benu's place to tell his children what he had done. Vera ran out to meet him but he was cold towards her.

I hear you now keep a gutter in your mouth.

No daddy, your wife was very mean to me.

No you haven't got any manners, you're just like your mother and I'm ashamed that I have a daughter like you.

Tears started to flow out of her eyes because she had never thought anything could have come between them. Her two brothers weren't in and neither was her mother, but she would later relate his message to them. They weren't invited to come and see him unless he asked for them. He looked around the small flat and saw his old dusty books sitting on a small shelf like splinters from a disaster. He winced at the editions of *Alice in Wonderland*, *Robinson Crusoe*, *My Life in the Bush of Ghosts*, *Bury My Heart at Wounded Knee* that all looked worn, dusty and uninviting. The reek of kerosene fumes was still there. The old gaudy painting of a White Jesus stood above the shelf without giving the impression of being able to work any miracles. On the rickety dining table, a few dirty dishes had a cloud of flies hovering over them. The unnecessarily huge television set stood like a grossly dated monument from another age. A smell of dirt rose out of the carpet. It was as if the whole flat was tired of carrying its own weight.

As Vera continued to weep quietly, her father left the forlorn flat without her seeing him off. In Vera's mind, he had committed the ultimate act of betrayal. But within his own eyes, he had done his wife's will, which was more important to him now.

Benu came back and found her only daughter crying. She was never one for sentimentality so she asked in a harsh tone what the matter was.

Daddy came here and insulted the whole of us. He said we shouldn't come to see him again just because of that whore.

Really?

Yes, Mummy.

Benu turned towards the shelf where the portrait of the White Jesus stood and addressed it:

Lord, you know I have done nothing wrong to Solo, yet he continues to humiliate me and my children. You know he doesn't wish us well and wants us dead. But let him be the one to die! Sweet Jesus, let that whore and her two spastic kids die the death of bastardy. And before this happens, Sweet Jesus, let my children and I see the light of victory before time runs out.

Her heart had sunk. Her hatred for Solomon had grown immeasurably. She had watched him grow into the man he was under her sweat and care. In the end he had turned out to be totally heartless, a monster. She let the hate run through her until her intestines twitched with pain. When she remembered what she had had to suffer through him during the time they were married, her veins stood out. Her temples bulged with blind rage. Evil was the word for him. Pure unadulterated evil was what she associated with him. She was convinced that he wanted her and her children dead. Once when they were still married and were having a fight, Solomon had snatched her panties and taken them to God knows where in his car. She kept screaming as she tried to climb onto the hood of his car whilst he drove off.

Solo, bring back my panties, where are you taking them to? Pervert.

He had taken the dirty ones. She shouted until their neighbours were drawn to the scene. What would he want to do with her underwear? they kept asking.

Benu was certain that it was for fetishistic reasons. She had been so sure that she had chased after his screeching car like a possessed woman. It was as if her life depended on it. She made many attempts to get on the hood of the car.

A few months later she started to bleed. She bled until she saw everything through the eyes and colour of blood. Everything smelt of blood too. When it struck her that she might die she told Solomon that she was bleeding. It's because we don't have sex anymore, he said.

They hadn't had sex for almost ten years. Solomon didn't particularly mind because there was another woman he was seeing. Usually his mood was easy because he was able to find ways to savour the afterglow of sex. A general suppleness held him together. She was, on the other hand, hardened from centre to edge. She became so taut, bones, nerves, tissues, glands, guts and all. No man would have her again. She had had all the children she wanted. She could do without sex and she didn't understand the point of having it if one had had enough children.

When Solomon saw that everything was tinted with her blood, that the arrogance of it was seeking to corrupt everything he called his own, he agreed to pay her hospital bills. Eventually she was treated, and for a couple of months she was fine.

When Solomon went on a trip to Oroke, something occurred again. Benu came down with a nervous breakdown. She had spent the whole of the May afternoon raving that her husband would die because he was a cruel man. Her friends had stopped coming to see her because all she ever talked about was that Solomon was going to die. Friends of her children would come and visit and she would preach to them that the wages of sin was death. The ones who shuddered amongst them told their parents who warned them never to go to Benu's house again. On the day she had her nervous breakdown, her menstrual period started. She started to live in the broken, tortured images of her past.

My children, you know I never beat you when you were young, unlike other parents who were so brutal to their kids.

She kept saying those words over and over again but her children knew they were lies. She had always been a terror to them. She made them undergo the harshest corporal punishments and never shrunk from using a stick on them.

Children, you know I never ordered you to stoop in punishment for hours in sweltering heat.

Of course she did. Her children understood that something was wrong when she didn't do something about the large patch of blood that had soiled her wrap behind. She kept calling her first son her husband and kept following him everywhere he went.

He is dead. He committed suicide by shooting himself, she would chuckle in a broken manner.

Benu went all about the house in the bloodied wrap saying Solomon was dead and asserting how much she loved her children. She didn't cook and none of her children could cook very well so they ate whatever crumbs they could find. Her memory came to her in broken bits. She called the television a computer that produced pictures that startled her. The brain was structured like a computer because of the way it produced sharp and disparate images and sensations.

My head is pick, picking up like the computer.

She snapped her fingers.

Solomon hadn't come and no one did either. Around the neighbourhood a word or two had gone round saying that

Benu was behaving strangely. The only thing she valued as much as her ruptured life was her money. Her children had hoped they would be able to take advantage of her breakdown to steal some of her horde but she had cleverly hidden it away when she started feeling funny in the head.

After several days the true names of things and people started to return to her. It was almost a miracle because she had received no medical treatment. Gradually her old recalcitrance and self-assurance returned. Her teeth began to gnash with the usual amount of rage. Vera started to receive the old stinging slaps from Benu. And the veil of prostrate blood was lifted from the troubled woman.

To a few who had heard the word, she had been tainted by madness. She had literally gone mad, but of course Benu could be trusted to defend herself to the death. Eventually the weed of the creeping rumour was choked to death. And it could only have been a rumour, after all she had her hard-swearing self again. Even to herself she never accepted the fact that she had suffered a nervous breakdown. That wasn't the problem. It was the symbol of evil that had hung over her like a baleful cloud in the figure of Solomon that was her problem. She hoped with the help of God he would come under the hand of death. As she thought about all what she had had to go through in the hands of Solomon, she was propped up by anger and regret. The fumes of her foul mood were the centre of her strength.

When Solomon returned home, he felt like a hero even though Tani did not openly treat him as such. He had done his part but she knew she would have to do hers in protecting herself and her children. No woman in her position could afford to sit like a lame duck on a seat of fat. There was work to be done. The following day she went to see her friend

Shadun so that she could be taken to see the spiritualist who would carry out the rites of protection.

I told you that you just can't sit still while your enemies remain unbound, said her friend.

Shadun was always willing to be of help to a friend who had access to higher circles. She saw her husband as a layabout and was sometimes ashamed of him. It was she who provided the greater part of the money for their upkeep. The money came from the affairs she had with the men Tani introduced to her. Her husband suspected this but did not mind as long as she gave him some respect. After a while, it all started to get into her head. But Bundu could not send her away. Indeed it was a thing of pride to have a wife who had one or two well connected friends.

There were a few birds hopping around the sinking slum. Behind, the lagoon stank like a corpse, but children swam far into it. Apart from simply swimming to enjoy themselves, they also hoped to catch mackerel. All the trees had been chopped down so the birds could only perch upon the tin roofs and electric wires. The miserable looking hovels hung like blighted ogres on a wrecked canvas. Tani walked through the slum with the carriage of a celebrity. She had had to park her car at a distance because it couldn't go any further. Boys and girls stood with hanging jaws ogling her freshness.

Shadun was ready in no time to take her friend downtown to the spiritualist's dwelling place. It was in another slum, right in the middle of the city. Drug addicts haunted the streets like keepers of the law. One had to give them money or suffer the displeasure of walking over them. There were innumerable little wooden kiosks that sold an assortment of wares: bales of cloth from India, vehicle spare parts from Belgium, Italian shoes, cheap T-shirts from China and Dubai, medicines and cheap electronics from Taiwan, *adire* from Abeokuta and wines from South Africa.

The spiritualist was a man of sixty or so. He had small shifty eyes that gave the impression of being well versed in the ways of evil as well as the concealed paths of life. He sat on a mat made of goat skin. He stank of sweat and raw tobacco and was bald. He related directly to Shadun and not to Tani, who needed his help.

What is the problem?

Tell Baba that I'm being disturbed by the foes of my home and that my husband does not love me enough, Tani said addressing Shadun.

Ha, that's a very common problem. In fact you're very lucky because I still have the supply of medicines for your problem."

How much will it cost?

Let's leave that till when it has worked, then you can give me whatever you think is my due.

As you wish, Baba, but I'm sure this is the beginning of what would be a fruitful relationship.

You children of today are always too much in a hurry, look at her already speaking of a relationship. Just look at her, what makes you think that I would even give you the medicines now!

Please, Baba we didn't mean it that way!

She already is talking of a relationship! Who told you I wanted a relationship with you? Your betters come here and I don't even attend to them.

Please, Baba, at least we have apologised.

Anyway, what makes you think that you can perform the rites?

She'll do anything you ask.

Let her not, it's her business.

Please, Baba. They both pleaded.

I will give you a powder, which you shall rub on your genitals before your husband makes love to you. Anytime he wants to have sex with you, you shall rub it finely around the edges. There is a potion you shall have to buy at the herb market nearby. Your friend shall show you. And then you shall buy a morsel of local soap she will also show you. You will bathe with it before you want to prepare your husband's meal. You will stand naked in a large cooking pot or basin and wash your body concentrating on your genitals. You will keep the used water and you will cook his meal with it. And then you will have the lobes of his brain between your thighs.

Thank you, Baba.

Both women knelt down in appreciation.

Outside, the sun sat in the sky like a fat fuming woman. The two friends got into their car and drove towards the herb market under the directions of Shadun. The market had the air of a subterranean tomb. The ground was murky with blood, rain water and mud. The men who sold their wares there looked like moody butchers. Some sold roots that looked like the wings of vultures. The twigs were more riotous than the hair of the insane. The goods were kept on rickety, old stained tables that swung with age. A few of the men sold the insufferably tough meat of old cows. Others sold camel, horse and donkey meat. Further on, more gory merchandise was on display. There were mounds of female breasts in their dried and fresh states. There were genitals of both sexes, dried and fresh. There were also human heads both male and female that kept endless waves of flies swinging about. At a dark end of the market, marijuana smoke was wafting. A train of well-dressed women kept coming and going. Presumably they were looking for money and being so hard to find, they had to do gory things to realise their wishes. The darkness crept like a royal serpent and evil swayed like a heavy listless whore. Finally the two friends got what they wanted from an albino and went outside, where the sun had fallen like a faded flower.

They drove to Tani's home cracking jokes all the while. Tani remembered the freshly cut human heads dripping with blood and her stomach turned. She couldn't believe that her friend visited such a dreadful place. Then she remembered the soap and potion that were meant to be panaceas for her, and her sense of fear and horror slowly evaporated. When they got home, she sent Lokoma to buy her friend some drinks. For hours they sat talking about the evil that men do until Tani got up to get dinner ready. As she left her glass behind, she whispered to Lokoma to keep an eye on it so that her friend might not try to poison her. Now that she had what she wanted she didn't even mind breaking up their friendship. After all she had nothing to gain from her now. Shadun's husband was just a poor insignificant bricklayer, while she had a bright future ahead of her. Soon after, Shadun left for her own home.

Tani sent her children to their bedroom. Solomon wasn't in the flat. She then put a potful of water on the gas cooker for her bath. The electricity was cut off. She lit a few candles and when the water was warm enough, she removed her clothes and washed herself, concentrating on her genitals, in the large pot. A storm was brewing outside and the candle in the kitchen flickered dead. Still it didn't start to rain. The generator in the next compound started with a grumbling din and a cone of light fell into her kitchen. Tani moved her bathing pot within the lighted cone and continued to bathe. When she had finished, she kept the water she had stored. The water that she had collected was now tainted with the secret potion. She lit the dead candles again and then it started to rain. Since water didn't run in the taps, she fetched all the buckets and cooking pots in the apartment and placed them on the edges of the roof, so rain water could fall into them. When she ran into the flat again, her wrap hugged her body like a film of snakeskin.

Solomon drove in as she was preparing his meal. By then the children had gone to bed. She had done as the spiritualist had instructed her.

God, the traffic was terrible, he said as he came in with a sprinkle of flake-like rain. He beamed to himself when he saw that the table had been laid. Tani went into the bedroom and changed into a pair of tights and a T-shirt. She didn't wear a bra. When he saw her, he knew he had to make love to her that night. The fried rice was much too greasy and had a lot of pepper, but he hadn't the courage to complain. He didn't want to spoil her mood for sex. He didn't bother to finish his meal before he dragged her into her bedroom where he hurriedly divested her of her clothes. She had managed to blow out the candle in the room. Solomon didn't see the white stuff that had been rubbed on her vagina as he struggled with the haste of a man of twenty-two out of his clothes. They made love once more before daybreak with Tani putting a leg lazily on the bedside table.

In the morning she made the usual breakfast of yam and eggs. The eggs were a bit too greasy and only half done. There were also a lot of unevenly chopped onions and tomatoes that tasted raw. Solomon had learnt not to complain anymore because of her tantrums. On that morning, though, he found a way of commenting harmlessly about her cooking.

You have a peculiar way of frying your eggs.

It's the water.

The water?

The water in the eggs.
Hmm.

He had never heard that fried eggs had any water in them.

The bottom has fallen out of the economy.

I know.

A basketful of tomatoes would fetch a pair of testicles.

Really?

I fried the eggs with a special kind of oil.

It must have been very expensive.

Are you kidding?

The yams are so hard.

That's because they are out of season.

And there is hunger in the land.

I'm glad you know that, so you can increase my housekeeping allowance.

But there's very little money coming in.

What would you like for lunch?

Rice and beans.
There isn't any oil in the house.

Is it finished already?

You gave me just enough money for a little.

Then I'll give you a little more.

It's better to buy in bulk.

I don't have enough money for bulk purchases.

You never have enough money for anything and yet you wouldn't allow me to find work.

A wife stays at home!

But only when the man can afford to keep the home and I'm getting tired of having to cook and clean the flat alone. It's too much for me.

In time, Solomon had come to realise that Tani wasn't just ill-bred, but that she was a bad cook as well. But he couldn't send her away even though they hadn't been married in a modern court of law. Their marriage had been contracted under native law and custom. He was proud of the fact that he had a woman whose sole purpose in life was to prepare his meals and lie in his bed. Even though her presence made him lose his elements he just couldn't send her packing. It would be an unbearable victory for Benu, whose sole wish in life was to see him fail in every sense. Tani's leaving would be her ultimate vindication. He wished he could endure her until he would be able to die in peace. But she was itching for the world that lay outside. She had sensed a longing for death creeping within him and didn't want to be a part of it. She had in her hands a weary old man and she hadn't plans to teach him the joys of life all over again. He would have to swim or sink on his own steam. He, too, had realised that she wasn't prepared to help him shoulder on. She was only in it for what she could get. They made no bones about erecting a facade of love. The harshness of their relationship stood starkly before them like shards of broken glass and the most they could do was gloss over it with the age old clichés of marital life. Time rolled on and their old positions merely hardened.

During the afternoon, an old friend came to see Solomon. She was a middle-aged woman whose husband had been his friend when he was married to Benu. Mrs. Farshi had been a really beautiful woman ten or so years before. Her husband had died about five years ago, after they had had to endure a bitter separation. They had fought each other fiercely using evil arts and Mr. Farshi had had to flee their house. When their marriage was still in a good shape, the Farshi and Wenku families were the best of friends. They went to exclusive clubs together, went to the movies and treated one another to picnics. At evenings, they would sit in their air-conditioned living rooms chatting and listening to Mozart and Vivaldi within plumes of Cuban tobacco smoke and a good bottle of brandy on the side. Those times were good and laughter ran like a river beside a cloister of bright young trees. They both had good jobs with a lot of perks to keep them happy. When they left their jobs, things began to change gradually. Benu began to find more reasons to hate Solomon and they tore each other apart until their fights exhausted all their strengths and they decided to part ways with a lot of hate still seething in them. The Farshis, too, tore at each other until the man went to his grave.

Benu and Solomon had been at his funeral, but they had gone separately. Mrs. Farshi received her condolences with a splendour that ran quite deep. Her eyes were dreamy and gentle and the men must have found her very desirable. Since the burial Solomon had not been to see her. When he saw her standing at the door of his flat, memory's dagger stuck him with incalculable force.

The peace of the Lord be upon this house.

She spoke in a voice as calm as the depths of old rivers. A thin smile had broken over her lips. She had become thinner since the last time he saw her, but she still looked very elegant.

Mrs. Farshi, good to see you… how are the children?

He saw her again sitting in his sitting room, Mozart wafting softly out of the stereo, her legs crossed and an enigmatic smile on her slightly parted lips. And it was that smile that hinted at the things she could do. She sat like the elder sister of Mona Lisa in the mild chill of air-conditioning, smiling-- half-puzzled-- at her husband's coarse jokes. Outside, night was re-living the memories of its virginity as the winds skipped over the heads of the sleeping plants. The snakes crawled out of their holes, crevices and other hidden places. A large reptile waited patiently for a stray chick. Night held itself to the moon's mirror face pretending to be young again. They had talked about the future and the night listened like a charming businessman whose real intentions one could not read.

Solomon looked at her and saw that time had played a cruel joke on her. Her newfound Christianity was a defence against the storms and heartbreaks that lurked around the living paths to her grave. Indeed everyone's grave. She, who had been a great party-lover, who sipped champagne with a special kind of panache, had had laughter snatched away from her. And instead of becoming hard and unresponsive to her pains, she had taken the other route to find a love that was of God and not of men. Solomon brought her into the living room and politely offered a chair. The furniture was coated with dust and he felt a slight pang of shame. The settee had grains of rice upon it. The poor taste of the décor was glaring to a person like Mrs. Farshi who had seen and lived in interiors that were created and handled by the finest imagination. She sat daintily and clasped her hands together while Solomon continued to fuss nervously over her. She had appeared to him like the keeper of the past's seal. When Tani saw her, she immediately perceived her as a threat whose charm her own vulgarity would be unable to match or annihilate. It annoyed her that she couldn't touch the visitor's charm and her hate grew even deeper. Mrs. Farshi sensed her hostility and her calm smile put on another shade that was neither under-stated nor accentuated, her smile acquired an added shade of mystery. Tani, with great verve, began to sing her religious songs. It was clear that they contained no love, that peace was far from her heart. Her songs were snatched along with her into the kitchen, and Solomon and Mrs. Farshi were left alone again.

You have a very young wife. Oh, it's been so long since we last saw each other.

Yes, yes.

Someone told me that you had married again, but somehow it didn't sink in.

What can a man do?

I am sure there is a lot he can do with the help of Jesus.

She had retreated from the issues with a sense of taste no one could fault. Tani came in again still singing her religious songs that had no love in them.

Lokoma!

Ma!

Bring your sick head over here!

The girl came and stood looking at her with fright in her eyes.

Did you sweep this place this morning?

Yes, ma.

You filthy dirty liar, she swore, throwing the broom she held in her hand at the child. It missed her and sailed just behind Mrs. Farshi's headgear. Solomon was embarrassed but he didn't say anything. He knew what was behind it all.

You filthy stinking swine! You'll see what I will do to you in this house! All you know is to eat. You can't even have your bath properly. Your entire body stinks.

She truly hated the child because Solomon hadn't really accepted her. The child on her part lived in fright and confusion. The only time she knew peace was when she was sleeping and even then she talked and jerked in her sleep. Once it was dawn, her terror began as she had to sweep and clean the entire place and then get ready for school. Tani treated her like an orphaned maid. Sukuma, on the other hand, was left to rot all in the name of a misshapen love. He followed his sister around like a tail, playing pranks on her and diverting her attention.

I'll get you today, monkey, she cursed again before she finally went back into the kitchen.

Something told Mrs. Farshi that it was time to go.

I came to invite you to a special breakfast meeting that would be held by my church and this is the invitation and…

I'm…

Don't worry, there would be no donations. We just want to create a forum for respectable men and women to meet and share the good things of the Lord. Our country is dying and those that would be saved are the children of Jesus. Look around the world today-- wars, starvation and disease. People dying by the thousands, everywhere, man has lost hope and only those who have Jesus are still protected. My children and I have come to realise His importance in our lives. We feel truly blessed. Please come, it's on Saturday. Come and be blessed, she said holding his hand. He felt uncomfortable and gently drew his hand away. Tani could have come in and misconstrued the gesture.

I'll try but I can't promise.

Please come.

As she got up to go, Solomon saw her down to her car. He was impressed with the way she carried her sadness. There was style to it, even though the clouds she emitted were ominous. Tani was still fuming when he came back inside. Lokoma was sweeping frantically to please her mother. Sukuma was lying on the couch with his legs spread apart and a finger in his mouth. Lunch wasn't ready. The air was strained with Tani's religious songs.

Daddy I want some ice-cream, Sukuma said running up to his father.

Not today, he said with a heavy spirit and went into his bedroom.

It was best to avoid Tani now that she was in a foul mood.

I spend my time shaking my arse around the place, sweeping and cooking your meals because you see me as some sort of slave and you only come and sit to eat. Lokoma! Get moving you monkey!

Solomon knew some of the remarks were directed at him. He had no strength to fight especially with someone whose heart had not only been poisoned, but hardened by rage. He was served no lunch and he didn't bother to ask. Tani was jealous of Solomon's past, jealous of the people he knew and the relationships he had formed. He had had to sink lower on the social scale to marry her but she didn't appreciate it. She reviled him instead. She wished she had lived with him through the bowels of time. In that way she would have complete mastery over him. She saw his past as a weapon although he hadn't intended it to be so. She lashed at the myths of his past, shattering its fine cobwebs, and its haunts of laughter. To her, it was sickening territory. Her vanity led her to construct tales to hide the impoverishment of her own past. Solomon always listened sympathetically, but that was not enough. He had to abolish his own past, he had to become a man without a history so that he could be perceived to be totally harmless. Solomon was even ready to do this impossible task, he was ready to refrain from referring to it. But the ghosts and points of light from the fragments of his past drifted towards him like shells pushed onto a beach by a sea. The buried tales rose from the dead, from lost and buried time spoke to him in Tani's presence. She always blamed him for these annoying intrusions as if he were responsible for the treachery. Her own past hung together like bits of hair from an artificial wig. It was a past filled with misery, squalor and violence and which needed to be suppressed or re-made. There was no meat in it, no vegetables either because that was where hunger resided. When the meagre totem of her past was held underneath the sun, the dryness of famine streamed through. This was why she was jealous of Solomon's relatively more bountiful past.

On the appointed day, Solomon didn't honour Mrs. Farshi's invitation. His fear of Tani hadn't allowed him and he sensed he was going to the past he knew. Mrs. Farshi had come to take him down the vegetative mists of a hidden future, one that was already in Tani's possession. And so he stayed at home.

That night he had a dream that terrified him. He saw Mrs. Farshi peeing, with a penis, in the toilet of the first flat in which he ever lived. She wore a blue house coat and her head was made up of squares. He couldn't tell if she had any breasts because of the size of the coat but it was certain that she had a vagina that pointed like a small snout. The bathroom had two doors, which were both opened and the two sons he had by Benu were drifting in and out. There were cries of little boys playing football beneath trees and the compound stank of corruption. Mrs. Farshi held on to her penis and continued to pee into his toilet. He didn't see Benu in the dream.

He woke up with a start and sweat had broken out of his body. He must have screamed because Tani was woken up too. But he felt too frightened to tell her about the dream because it was certain to infuriate her. He thought the dream came as a result of not honouring Mrs. Farshi's invitation. After that, the memory of the dream never left him. He carried it with him to his grave. He couldn't understand how Mrs. Farshi could have appeared so horrific to him. Although she had been beautiful, he never harboured any desires for her. She was a good friend's wife and that was all. The only relationship to which he felt an obligation was with her husband who was now long dead. The dream made him think that the dead man was watching over him from wherever he might be. He had always felt a vague bond between him and the dead man, a feeling that their souls might probably sail towards the same realm. He couldn't understand why he dreamt about his wife. But he believed the heartbreak she caused him had sent him to an early grave. The incident told him that he couldn't abolish his past no matter how hard he tried and in spite of Tani's efforts. He had been a fool to even try. There was no point in flaunting it before her, he couldn't even afford to but he wasn't going to chase after it again with the purpose of destroying it. He had become too exhausted to battle effectively with ubiquitous shadows.

Images of blood and death flitted back to him. He remembered one Christmas season when his family had gone to one of the old colonial parks that was in front of a lagoon. It was a large lovely park that had lots of pines. The lagoon had long poles that had been put there by foreign fishermen. The roots of trees ran all over the park grounds. Almost everyone seemed to have a music box. Dance music from innumerable stereos blared like distress calls. People danced until clouds of dust were flitting everywhere. Many got drunk, and lovers made love behind trees. Men fought each other over women.

Solomon remembered a particular fight. Two men were exchanging blows with a tree standing between them. The weaker man started throwing dust into his opponent's face to obstruct his vision. Then the blurry-eyed man got even angrier and brought out a knife and went through the dust into the other man's flesh. The blade caught him in the stomach and he bled to death beside the tree as revellers hurried home past him. His eyes rolled inwards, showing only the whites and he couldn't call out for help. No one stopped to give him a hand and when enough air had gotten into his large wound, he breathed his last by the tree whose roots ran over the ground like monstrous claws.

Solomon and Mr. Farshi got drunk on that night playing the symphonies of Beethoven endlessly. They wanted to destroy the memory of the dead man's ordeal with the force, vastness and imagination of the composer. As they left the park, the breezes from the lagoon mingled with the beginnings of dusk. The breezes twisted sadly and leisurely like an old female dancer executing her final steps before she entered into the shrine of honour. Death, blood and the smell of dusk kept coming back with quiet tales of horror. The sweat of nostalgia covered Solomon. It was the sweat he hated the most with its clammy feeling and malarial colour. As he remembered the blood that leaked out of that tragic Christmas evening, sadness sat upon the air like a monarch issuing out numerous decrees with the insouciance of a power drunk tyrant. Sadness continued to saunter about like grey rumours of death.

Soon after, yet another indispensable figure from the past cropped up in Solomon's life. He received word that Mrs.

Amoo's mother was dead. Faldaya Amoo had been Solomon's best friend before he died in a car crash many years before. They had grown up together running around the in wilds and farmsteads of Oroke. They had simply been inseparable all through their early lives and through school. And they had gotten married almost at the same time. Solomon to Benu and Faldaya to Feyimi, whose mother had just died.

When Faldaya died, Solomon had had a short-lived affair with Feyimi. Benu had been away to pay her mother a visit when Feyimi came to spend her period of mourning with the Wenkus. She had been put up in the master bedroom and Solomon transferred to the children's room. Feyimi had brought her two children with her and they too slept in the same room with her. During the day, all the children would be out playing. They hadn't known the meaning of death beneath the pines through which sunrays shimmered along with their ricocheting cries. The dawn of their first happiness was still roaming over virgin fields uncorrupted by the pains of adulthood. At bedtime, they returned completely exhausted and slept all through the night oblivious of the burning questions that looked like figures in mourning behind the retinas of first joys.

Feyimi was filled with sorrow and was soaked with mourning. Her body withered slowly and her days made her giddy. Solomon could see that her body was no longer hers. Her spirit laid somewhere else, the loss of her husband had meant a certain loss of sense, of feeling. She was a plank that could be walked on, a body to be used.

When she slept, she covered her body with a single sheet. The adjoining door to the children's bedroom was always open. She always seemed to sleep very lightly, unlike her two little children who never budged until the morning's light brightened up the room. The first few nights she spent in the flat were unbearable for Solomon. Sorrow had made her irresistibly alluring. Her body was an open forest without thorns, or at least his lust blinded him to the thorns.

On the third night, he could not resist the temptation to venture into her room. He wanted to make love to her without him or her uttering a word. He wanted the whole of their joint vocabulary to be encompassed by their lovemaking. As it was, she too had been expecting him. Intuition had told her that he longed for her even before the death of her husband. And yet to her, he just wasn't there, she could never have gone to him because her world floated where he could never venture. He might have understood that world because if he didn't, he would never have attempted to violate her so brazenly. Her world had no doors- it just strayed in time floating in the mists of a selfless acceptance. Morality was non-existent there, and anger broke under the scrutiny of light.

But she uttered some words on the first night he had sex with her:

This is not good for us.

Solomon grunted all the way through. What was good and what wasn't? Lust never had time to decide. What was good was the flow of seed to the banks of exhaustion. What was good was the crack of guilt on a mirror. What was good was naked flesh contemplating the vanity of rumpled clothes on the floor.

After that, their lovemaking became a matter of routine. She might as well have given herself to him like a blouse. She had been as available as that simple but loaded act. The only time she showed any irritation was when she needed to wander into private reveries, which was akin to washing her blouse. Solomon did not seem to mind dirty blouses. She was the large naked arm floating in the clouds, which he pursued with a prick. And he pursued the silent music of her floating away, he followed the endless drift to nowhere.

The death of her husband had exposed her to vast continents of loss against which she couldn't struggle. Solomon was just a noisy speck of rain in that loss. Then he became a storm she couldn't discard and he became the naked truth to be found in a sunray.

As her children grew, there were school fees to be paid, there were hospital bills to be settled, there were countless necessities that demanded attention and many obligations to be honoured. It was then she saw Solomon in the naked truth of a ray. She was stung by the absence of dream, by the unimaginativeness and lack of beauty life can sometimes acquire, by the destruction of nuance and feeling. She needed Solomon as a mediator in that void of fire and emptiness that stretched out before her as the path of life.

Solomon got the message in a hotel suite out of town. She offered herself to him formally as a mistress. The glass she drained of its soft drink content had lipstick stains all over it. Nothing could have symbolised more aptly the gift of herself to him. The sunlight streamed into the suite with expansive obscenity. Solomon had worn a dark Spanish suit. She had a bright floral dress on. He sat on the edge of the bed while she paced about the room. Her voice meandered like a light echo as she clasped her hands together. Many floors below, there were noises of splashing water in the swimming pool. A lot of Europeans sat around the pool sunning themselves out.

They made love once more and she cried again "please help me and my children". Her pleas had stripped her of the purity of sorrow. She immediately shrunk to the size of a clan filled with all the inadequacies of its corruptions. She became circumscribed in his eyes. In his eyes, she had acquired the narrowness of a small stone. Those words of hers seemed dead to the world of dreams. They were unresponsive to adventure. There isn't any poetry in a brick wall except when it is washed by rain or speckled with moss or sadness. She had suddenly become objectified, sterilised by the naked activity of survival.

After that, their lovemaking took on a new meaning. It now had the banality of stones, steel and rainless times when everything had to have a definite meaning. Perhaps the widest meaning is contained in the state of meaninglessness within which she had reeled when Faldaya was alive. All around, acts rebounded upon the surface of the sun with an unreality incapable of the pleasure of drowning. Solomon had been attracted to her because she embraced the purest ethic of the drowning soul. She once embraced the clouds or sunk into the depths of an ocean. She emanated a poetry no one could touch and which very few could see. He was among the few who saw it. But she had now renounced all those powers. The deed of reading the stark colours of a dress, the relentless search for ontology had taken all her poetry away from her. But she had taken the easier way out for the sake of her children and the dictates of the forest where life evolved in all its simplicity and majesty. The jungle law says eat and procreate. With animals this law never loses its majesty but under the same law, the lives of men appeared to be a language without a lush tongue or fire without its uneven spark.

Solomon stopped seeking her out and avoided her when she sought him. She sent him a letter to which he never replied.

During vacations, she took the children to spend some time with the Wenkus, but he was always so businesslike. The barrier he had erected between them seemed so ludicrous having plunged in the same stream together so many times. Later she got the message and stopped bothering to check up on him.

During her mother's wake-keeping, Solomon turned up wearing the dust of age. Although he wasn't exactly a poor man, his fortunes had gradually decreased. Since they parted, she had had affairs with wealthier men who stood by her. Solomon came thinking he could reclaim old territory, but she received his hug as if it were a wet towel. The wake-keeping took place on a narrow side-street. Women made up most of the sympathisers. Most of the women were middle-aged or old. Solomon sat at the edge of the congregation with a younger cousin. The booklets of the programme and songs had been borrowed from a recently bereaved family because there wasn't enough money to print new ones. The banality of the rites was so gloomy. It seemed worse than death, which had an indivisible finality, a separateness which cannot be altered or repeated. Repeating the same old solemn hymns was bad enough, but the tragedy was doubly perceived when one had to sing from a borrowed and inappropriate hymn book. The readings from the Bible that stank of an unending death, the yawns of the old knowing their own end would soon come and the predictability of the officiating priest's voice; all these factors widened the chasm between the living and the dead. It was a keen longing for the bean cakes that awakened the taste for life before the weakness of death started to overpower the living again.

After the service, old friends gathered to exchange greetings. It was more like comparing notes. Solomon had very little to show for himself. Benu had divorced him and he had taken an ill-bred hag for a second wife. His finances weren't exactly admirable. His old friends and acquaintances dredged up his past and the pain was unbearable. No one had exactly referred to it but seeing them again was such a torture. Their respectable voices, though subdued, swished like whips in the air of his past. He could not bear the sight of old families that had weathered storms to become as established as wall-geckos. He felt like a worthless prodigal. He had wilfully extinguished the promise that life had held out in his dawn. His old acquaintances stood talking about nothing in particular apart from making slight, deft forays into the past. It remained like one of the pigeons flying through a grey sky with strips of satin in their beaks. It conveyed such a powerful impression of lost charm.

When can one reach you, Solo? said a man who was a top civil servant.

You better give me your card and I'll reach you.

But you never turn up, you always seem to be in hiding.

Of course I'll drop by to see you.

Make sure you do.

Solomon was glad to have gotten rid of him. He summoned his cousin and escaped from the crowd of old acquaintances. He realised that a cloud heavier than death hung over his head. His marriage to Tani was in some ways a severance from his past because she loathed it. And the figures from it fed on nostalgia, which his present could not tolerate. He drove into the night with bitterness in his gut and mouth. Feyimi had triumphed over his insensitivity on the night that it mattered the most because the past had vindicated her.

Oroke so far away. Over one hundred years ago, the little clan grazed the surrounding the hills trying to protect a fragile innocence. The clan finally lost its glory when bands of savage warriors combed its interior, hauling away several able bodied men as slaves. They were held in rusty chains on blood soaked evenings. The bare breasts of young girls huddled together like resigned beasts that couldn't speak of all their sorrow. Nor could the dry jaws of old men chewing roots and watching in quiet wonder. Neither could the discomfiture of frightened hunting dogs who held the smell of death in their noses. Oroke had conceded to lie with defeat, something that was never washed out of its collective throat. Those who became wise started by understanding the uses of power. Solomon's great-grandfather had been among the first to undergo the bitter training. His grandfather converted to Christianity at the age of twelve, making him a pioneer. It was when the inhabitants of the village turned their backs to the hills that the language of metal began to harden their bones.

Solomon had been among the early beneficiaries of western education. As he progressed, he became admired by everyone. He did as he wished and no one bothered him. Once he had an affair with the young wife of an old man. The old man had blessed the relationship implicitly. Solomon would visit his lover at sundown, when the old man sat in his veranda drinking palm wine. He would wink at his young man and usher him in to where the woman who was their link was waiting.

Would you be able to come and see me tonight? he would ask her when he was ready to leave.

Usually she was able to come and they would make love for a couple of hours until it was time for her to return home. She would arrive with a potful of warm water for him to have his bath and a bowl of food. No one frowned at their relationship which flowered in his hut. But he always warned her to be respectful to her aged husband.

He's a foolish old man, she would say.

But he's still your husband.

He is useless.

Give him respect.

The hut that served as their meeting place was usually dark and unlit. They wanted it so.

One day Solomon was going out to drink with his friends when he saw her verbally abusing her husband. He stood beneath a tree in the dark listening to them quarrel.

Better shut your mouth or else I'll shut it for you.

If you lay a finger on me I'll lay twenty on you! Shameless old man.

I can see you don't have any respect for your father.

Then why did you marry his daughter?

I was blind then, I can see I've made a big mistake.

You've always been a blind fool.

Shut your mouth, I say.

Shut your mouth, too!

When Solomon could take it no longer, he emerged from the dark and gave her a slap.

Haven't I told you not to disrespect Baba? he yelled at her.

She started to cry and went inside her hut. The old man pulled him aside and thanked him profusely for saving him from her wrath. After that, he began to respect Solomon even more.

Goats scratched their flanks against the rough walls of mud huts and the rains fell according to the turn of the seasons. Other women crashed into Solomon's life like waves and disappeared soon after when he left the confines of Oroke. Benu succeeded in locking herself in his heart when she saw he was a cloud that carried no name. She stayed there until his namelessness began to reply her shouts and tantrums. When she left, his namelessness got reinstated once more. He then married Tani, who was still very young and smelt of the woods. The odour became coarse and unbearable when she stood up fiercely to deny it. She climbed on to a pedestal above him and spat on his head and he began to experience his old sorrows anew. Their two children were born, but she wanted more so she would have earned her right to stay. Solomon had become sick of having children, but the other option was having to face the desolate dusk at the end of his life alone. Tani was the noise he acquired to fill that terminal void.

****

Twenty-two years later when he was sixty-two, he learnt a shattering secret. Feyimi had had a son for him. He felt an outpouring of guilt. He also felt like a void-bearing chariot. The son, Ayimola had tormented his mother until she revealed his father's name. When he turned up at his door, Solomon immediately saw his own face staring out to him and he immediately understood everything. He had no choice but to take him into his home. He lied to Tani that he was his nephew. Later on, she got to know the truth but kept quiet.

Ayimola was a gifted artist. He had started off by writing poems and he loved to lie by the radio all day long. Solomon used to think that he was lazy until the young man started to receive a lot of media attention by virtue of poems he had written. A pop group had converted his poem into a hit song titled *Swing*:

Thinking 'bout thinking
All about doing
From Jazz to arse
It's the same shit
Harlem or Berlin
You just have to make the hit
Now you clock the gist
It's a game without a plan
Coming out of history it's called
With an eye for

The white-haired Sephardic Jew
So make it swing from
Jack to the New City
I'm the man with Time's
Needle up the arse
I ate the world's balls
To be the life
I chopped off low boobs
To step into the dance
Come on give me a band
Hold up the trophy.

Ayimola set up a commune of artists where Bartok, Parker and Coltrane were listened to and wine was drunk and weed smoked. He composed some other poems, which he read to his fellow artists with a low voice:

By His Good Lord
Bones turn to jelly ruins
Is my front
Want to be my all
And for me now
There is no house to turn to
Before me is my Lord
Whose bones are newly delivered
Wet with a soft voice
Which I wish could be burning mountains
It is my life of soft bones
Dripping with a voice
I cannot hear
That I wish would splinter the woods

Meant for thunder and fire
Voice of streams where we've rinsed our feet
Don't sing!
You urge it to go there
And it slumps in an expanse of mud
Tired of the strength it can't dream of
Wet bones whence my lord is made
Find the voice of your wood
Lest I find mine
Batlike cloud when would you hold
Unto a pole of eminence?
Or would you forever remain something
Unconnected to being?

Bare Shrine

And in the plain village square
Under the flirtatious moon, loveless
They draw out their horns of age
First for the wine
And then the verdict.
All within the dual nature of kola
The horns in those ghastly hands
That rose out of an enormous womb
On a misty morning
Draw the uncleared paths before young feet
Elders your son is dancing
In a bare shrine
Reading the cobwebs, in a boneless sanctuary
Flesh alone is talking elders
He is creating electric suns
Where thighs flail.

Fear

A broken spine of iron
Shaking fragile teeth
To its most chilling music…
Tremors in the brain without cancer
But a swinish whine in man
Gathering the tremulous jaw
In singular confinement
And the lights in spite of the pain
Oblique sunshafts on a bloodless wound
The lights stringing the music to the teeth
But for the shutters of the room
That safeguards the spy
The guardian shadows, refuge
From the nakedness in the sun.

Ayimola stopped writing poetry when he wrote this poem of hate.

Trout Face

Trout face who we made
From the curve in a bow
The string at the ready
On electric poles
Singing his obstinacy out in fangless air
At the beginning no shadows were bled
Likewise at the end, no shadows
Trout face with whom we kept
The accursed tongue
He would have us believe
He is wine's best friend
He would station himself ahead of the seer
Emperor who thinks he has

The silvery tongue
Let it be said
That he was sired by a boar!
Rampaging in the bars, an exposed brain
Trout face who swallowed
The accursed tongue.

Ayimola swore never to write any other poem. He even resolved to burn all the poems he had written. Then he decided he wouldn't burn them, instead, he would send them down a river, the same river that Benu had offered her gourds.

Three female poets accompanied him on the evening he decided to make his offerings of creativity. The wind was the drummer and the flutist. The three poets wore long transparent skirts made from nylon. Their figures flapped in the wind like apparitions. As Ayimola sat in lotus position watching the motionless brown body of water before him, the poets started a well crafted voluptuous dance that made them seem like delicate tongues of fire in the wind. When the wind started threatening to eat up their figures, he threw his creativity into the river. The lifeless sheets of paper bore no marks of his intensity. They all watched the sheets of paper sailing in water at the end of their impersonal journey. After that, all the poems he had inside him he uttered or lived through in real life. The poets continued to meet inside a fine bamboo shed that was fringed with coloured bulbs. Caribbean-like tunes usually wafted out of the wings. Beer and wine mellowed their sorrows and the palms swished through the passage of the evening. Ayimola had a dream to share, one that he narrated like a prose poem:

The world was harsh and intractable. The sun stuck out like a curse. History shone like an eternal virgin and the present trudged on in its vomit. The days were hard and blood lost its lyre. Socrates established himself in the present because he wanted to prove it could be endured. He sat in the middle of the most crowded market place beside a traffic-laden causeway. Hawkers combed the length and breadth of the causeway between the endlessly prowling vehicles, the air heavily polluted by exhaust fumes. Socrates had a cream coloured cloth around his body and was eating a loaf of bread and bean cakes. He had overturned one of his central tenets, because perhaps he lived to eat, after all what was there to do? The sun hung buzzing with its sting and bodies went to and fro in various stages of disintegration. Treated hair wilted in the heat. Bodies whose treachery weren't covered by clothes walked on by. They already smelt of their dusk, their final decay and when they still seemed like bright flowers, they looked as if they were waiting to be cut down. Virtually no one paid the great sage any attention. He became as familiar as numerous mentally ill men who pursued their fractured dreams to death. He kept on talking about knowledge, which he didn't use. His words ventured into the smoke-filled air and dropped like meaningless objects. Then the fair and handsome Alcibiades appeared. He had come to invite Socrates to a party. Socrates was reluctant to go because there was so much vanity in such parties. Alcibiades's body grew soft as he slumped to the feet of the master who remained adamant in his refusal. Socrates continued to churn out his silent thoughts like grains and Alcibiades began to sing dulcet lullabies. Pedestrians continued to stream past them almost oblivious of their presence. The glare of the sun began to shimmer. Try as it may, the city could not recapture the feel of old romance, the few trees that remained had become covered with vehicular smoke. Houses had risen everywhere like standing cadavers. Violence forever stalked the ugly byways like unrepentant demonic snakes. Shed blood was left to turn black. Corpses that had been hitherto beautiful were left to decay and stink. The black mouths of the dead opened to the waxing strength of the evening and prostitutes daintily stepped over them in high-heeled shoes to ply their trade. Rain water muddied by black mud stank in the alleyways.

Alcibiades had taken off his clothes and was still sitting at Socrates feet.

"Fuck me, old sage" he said to the pensive Socrates. Socrates kept silent and his young friend began to rub the soles of his feet. When he was tickled, Socrates would withdraw his feet sharply. Alcibiades' hands moved upwards and began to rub the bulge in Socrates' crotch.

"Don't be a spoilt sport, fuck me," he continued to say. The sage persisted in forming his thoughts in his head but they had none of their usual fluid arrangement. Alcibiades was clearly in his mind. His breathing grew wild and uneven. Blood rushed to his temples. His thoughts were overmastered by one long rush of lust. Alcibiades figure slithered like a seductress in his field of vision. When he saw that the violence of his panting could be harmful to him, Socrates dragged his tormentor underneath a nearby bridge and unscrewed his prick which he promptly inserted into his Alcibiades' bum. The prickless Socrates walked back to his concrete block while Alcibiades wriggled with pleasure, cock in bum. Thank you". The moral of the poem, if your cock torments you, unscrew it!

A chorus of clapping ensued. The dream had conquered the poet. Ayimola's fame spread, but he refused to write any more poetry.

Ayimola spent his days lying beside the radio waiting for more dreams to take him. Tani had him in mind and wanted to be his only dream. She still hadn't had another child and was beginning to doubt Solomon's potency. Ayimola looked exactly like his father and Tani had begun to nurture the idea of having a child by him. When Solomon was away, her body openly invited Ayimola. He ignored all the signals. And then she told him frankly that she desired him. He was simply confounded, his father's wife pleading with him to take her to bed. The struggle went on until he couldn't resist her implorations any longer. She had cornered him on the day that they were alone. The blinds were drawn and the darkness seemed to tingle an almost perceptible mischievousness. Tani took off her clothes and laid on the couch like an artist's model. Her smell suffused the room. Ayimola sat regarding her with a cold eye. Her impatience began to tell on her face and body. He moved to the couch and sat beside her. The look of expectation gave her eyes an unusual allure. He regarded her pubic hair and then stroked it. Her body almost folded in with pleasure, Ayimola put his head between her thighs and myriad visions swept through him. He kept seeing his father's limp penis nodding like a puppet. Each time he stroked her hair, he saw a dead black dog lying beside a huge snake, which was in the process of devouring it. He continued to stroke her and her pleasure grew. But he made no attempt to take off his clothes. Each time he looked through her, he saw a dark deserted tunnel filled with black hair. He also saw immobile bristles that had the silence of graveyards. He continued to stroke her until she reached a climax. After that, her desire died and he gained his freedom. Her desire took a turn slowly like a planet and wore another shade and still she didn't have a child.

****

Solomon continued to wait for the high point of his dusk to engulf him. There were few distractions for him now. He went for a walk one night and saw a house burning. People were screaming and trying to put out the fire with little buckets of water. The fire, which had started in one flat in the building, was threatening to spread to other apartment blocks. Cars were broken into and pushed outside the compound away from the inferno. Petty thieves snooped around hoping they could steal something but the vigilance was rigorous. Solomon helped in pushing some of the cars to safety. Eventually when the fight was getting in favour of the fire someone rode on a motorbike to a nearby fire station. The firemen agreed to come after much pleading and bribes. They sped down to scene in their ramshackle trucks and trained their hoses on the inferno. A sigh of relief swept through the spectators. After a while the firemen went away and the fire started to flare up again. Once more, a motorcyclist was sent to fetch them. And again, they had to be implored and bribed before they accepted to offer their services. But this time, they succeeded in putting out the fire for good. Solomon walked home slowly thinking of the loss and hardship the fire victims would have to bear.

Tani began to get jealous of Ayimola's continued stay in her home, so she sent word to her younger sister, Wandu, who was in her early twenties, to come and live with them. She also knew Wandu's presence would relieve her of her numerous household duties. Soon after, Tani put a pot of meat on the gas cooker and went into her bedroom to lie down. She slept off and when the water in the pot dried up, the meat started to burn. Solomon smelt charred meat from the landing and rushed into the kitchen to turn off the cooker. Fuming, he went to wake Tani up.

I know you're intent on burning this house down! You always do this, why must you make this a habit?

Can't I get any peace in this house? Must I be the one to do everything?

You're the woman of the house.

And what do you the husband do? Lazy old man. He goes about looking for burnt pots in the kitchen while his mates go out to make money. You should be ashamed of yourself.

What I'm telling you is that you're going to burn this building down!

What kind of man is this? I can't believe a man prays to be visited by fire. Use your mouth in bringing a curse upon yourself.

You're so unteachable. It was a big mistake marrying you.

Then marry another wife so that the world would see how useless you are, she said raging out of the bedroom.

Lokoma! Lokoma!! Wandu!!

Lokoma and Sukuma were playing downstairs. The little girl came running up the staircase and ran into a barrage of blows. Lokoma's cries were poignant beneath the continuous cursing of her mother. She made neither lunch nor dinner that day and for one whole week the flat stank of charred meat.

You child of wood, she continued to call Lokoma. She fed Lokoma on the sly but completely ignored the girl. The following morning, Wandu, who did not know of the quarrel prepared breakfast for Solomon who was relieved to assuage his hunger. Feeling good, he left the flat to prolong his peace.

Wandu! Tani shouted when Solomon had gone, who told you to give that bastard food?

Your husband?

Yes, the bastard.

You call your husband a bastard?

It's none of your business what or who he is-- just answer my question.

What's wrong about getting your husband food?

What's wrong? You want to steal my husband from me, is it so?

That's very unfair!

But that's what you girls of today do, you go about stealing other people's husbands.

I don't have to take this from you!

Shit? Did I hear you say shit? I'm talking shit, is it so? You're leaving today. I can't tolerate a rude spoilt girl like you around.

I'm neither rude nor spoilt.

Would you stop talking back at me?

Then keep your tongue in your head.

You are still talking? Look, I will beat the shit out of you if you over-step your bounds.

If you lay a finger on me, I won't stand watching.

Shadun came in and sat at the dining table. Her pleas for the altercation to stop were only half-hearted, or perhaps she had become too weary from coping with her own petty daily struggles. Tani served her a bottle of beer and continued to exchange hot words with her sister.

I'm warning you shut your mouth, you hear, you rat.

I am not a rat.

In fact you're worse than a rat! I don't care that we emerged from the same womb! You're a disgrace! A worthless husband-snatcher.

The cheek, trying to steal my husband from me? I don't know who asked you to prepare him a meal in the first place.

You're just an ingrate.

What? Me an ingrate? You're a shameless whore and till the day of your death no man shall take you in his house, you shall die alone and you shall never know the warmth and understanding of a man. That's a curse upon your head.

Tani spat on the floor and stepped on it. Wandu began to cry. Shadun was still making half-hearted pleas for them to stop their quarrel. Wandu went into the children's bedroom and started to gather her things in a bag. Crying, she went through the door and vowed never to come back. Tani became very suspicious of people and her phobia that Shadun was trying to poison her grew worse.

With her sister gone, Tani decided to employ a young steward who would help her with the chores. Ayimola hadn't been particularly helpful because he was always hanging out with poets and painters.

The steward she got was called Otabolo. Otabolo loved to dance and was a cheerful young man. The children liked him and never left him alone. He slept in the sitting-room and became quite friendly with Ayimola. Nights, they would share cigarettes. Twelve-year-old Lokoma fell madly in love with him although he was much older than her, being twenty-five. He filled her with a deep feeling for laughter. She would climb onto his back and when she had the chance she would try to pull him down to the floor. Later they developed a strong physical attraction for each other. Otabolo was very circumspect, he made sure no one suspected anything. Lokoma would rub his crotch with her small delicate fingers. He knew what she wanted but he bided his time. Being a clever man, he knew his future and security were at stake.

Meanwhile, their games continued. Tani usually gave Lokoma her dirty underwear to wash. Sometimes her panties were caked with menstrual blood. Lokoma couldn't understand it and Otabolo explained it to her. Tani persisted in calling her daughter a filthy pig. Once she saw a streak of shit on one of the panties and showed it to Otabolo.

She calls me a filthy pig, swine and whatnot now look at this. Who's the filthy one?

Otabolo merely laughed and Lokoma went off to wash off the dirty panties in her happy-go-lucky way. They were always having a laugh at Tani's expense.

Tani would call for Otabolo sprawled naked on her bed and ask him to fetch her clothes from the wardrobe. He never failed to be baffled. She would send for him to come and flush the toilet after she had used it. As there was usually scarcity of water, they often had to make do with the rainwater they had collected in containers placed below the roof. Lokoma and Otabolo would laugh until tears came to their eyes. Sukuma was too foolish to understand what was going on.

One day, Otabolo disvirgined Lokoma when both Tani and Solomon had gone out. Sukuma had been very tired and had fallen asleep. She had experienced so much pain that Otabolo had to carry her to bathroom where he washed her and then had taken her to the bedroom where she laid with her legs held tightly together. He was afraid she wouldn't be able to bear the pain and confess what had happened, so he bought her some painkillers and sweets. She accepted what he offered and laid shivering slightly on the bed. When her parents returned, she lied that she had a bout of malaria, but Tani decided that it was her filth that had made her ill. After a couple of days, the girl was fine again. Her first taste of sex had badly shaken her and she didn't want to repeat it. Otabolo was scared, so he constrained himself to touching and fondling her.

Ayimola was quietly thinking about what direction to turn his creativity. Photography struck him as a very interesting medium. He acquired a camera, but he had still not found a motif. Walking through a street that was flooded with rainwater one afternoon, he noticed refuse chaotically littered around overfilled decrepit bins. Flies buzzed endlessly over the sickening array of rotten vegetables, stale grains of rice, torn plastic bottles, dirty mangled cellophane bags, scraps of metal from discarded electronic wares and other household appliances, banana and plantain peelings, soiled cartons and dead rats. The flies continued to get busy. Some of the refuse floated in the flood in the street. The stench hung in the air like a pointed gun. In front of every house, there was the same disorder created by stinking garbage. In the air, there was the same interminable buzz of flies. And then an idea struck him. He would begin to take photographs of the little garbage dumps he came across and place them right beside the stinking original shapes. He was really intrigued by the shapes and sizes of the dumps. No matter how riotous they appeared to be, they seemed to be able to capture a symmetry that was innate to themselves. By employing an appropriate feel of the eye, they could be transformed into *objects d'art.* Ayimola started to do what his creative urges told him. He puzzled everyone. Though many made their living rummaging in garbage dumps, the idea of taking photographs of them was not only novel but also bizarre. The puzzlement increased when he started to place the developed pictures by the dumps. Anyone was free to take them if they wished. Ayimola called his project, *Giving Art to the People.* He acquired notoriety and then once again fame. Reporters followed him everywhere asking him questions about his project and artistic ideas. The intellectuals had a lot of problems pigeonholing him. His art seemed immediately petit bourgeois, impossibly abstract, elitist and intolerably self-indulgent. But then he subverted these categorisations by placing it at the disposal of the people. Money was the last thing on his mind and then, unexpectedly, he began to receive commissions. Literary and artistic journals commented on, and featured his works extensively. Some critics construed his efforts as urgent pleas to save the environment. His art was a mirror held up to the destruction of the natural world by the excesses of commerce and consumerism. He had clearly come of age as an artist and almost overnight he became a much talked about figure.

Tani grew jealous. She wanted her son to become significant too so when it rained, she gathered the water and sprinkled it over his head. It was meant to bring good luck. The rest of the rainwater she sprinkled around the flat to drive away evil spirits. When Solomon travelled to Oroke for a short holiday, she invited a few Christian spiritualists to spend the night praying for her and her children. She asked the spiritualists to offer prayers so that she could become wealthy. The men wore long white robes with red sashes around their waists. Before they commenced praying for her, Tani gave them a meal of rice and fish. They lit candles all over the entire flat. By dawn, when they finished, the now dead candles had burnt holes into the carpets.

Solomon came back and saw the back of his night inexorably approaching. Tani stood firmly back refusing to venture forth with him as he expected a wife would. She was still evolving within the moment of dawn. Her own innate energies were only beginning to be aroused. She hadn't even experienced enough of the glitter of life.

Solomon recalled that ten years before his father had died. He was deemed to have died a good death. He had been quite respected in his village and everyone had turned out for his burial. They spent a few nights singing songs of praise to God and the dead man. And when they carried his casket to the grave, all the villagers trooped out. There were cries of loss, joy and gratitude that made an impressive cacophony. He had felt proud when he threw a shovelful of dust into the grave. He had been happy to be a son of a man who everyone wanted as a father. He knew there would be nothing special about his own burial. He remembered Mr. Farshi and the blood soaked Christmas evening at the park. He recalled his vile betrayals and his irreparable estrangement from Tani whom he had been foolish enough to give a chance.

His financial position worsened and then he suffered a stroke. Tani nursed him for a while until she got tired. She kept on grumbling that an old man was enough headache but an ill old man was intolerable. She left him one afternoon sitting naked by the window shouting at passersby for help. Two years later, Solomon Wenku died in a hospital heart-broken, unmourned and alone. His death was nothing like his father's. His father's life and death recalled and represented another era, a different season of values marked by a pronounced communalism. Solomon had yearned for that unifying spirit of communal values. He had seen many climes and had seen times change but he refused to acknowledge the passing away of old seasons and the comforts they brought. He had thought he had a right to enjoy those comforts. Alas he was wrong. The mere fact that he had seen and experienced many other climes and times had separated him from his father. Solomon came from a polluted, rather, a diluted world in which the disconnection of modern life would have to be faced alone. Here, the hug of death was both bitter and tasteless. Here, death discards its human embrace and connects instead with its endless and ultimate starkness with no ceremony.

Part II

Tani went to Oroke for Solomon's burial. It didn't go as well as one would have wished. It was fortunate he had a little bungalow on the outskirts of the village. The villagers weren't too pleased about it. It was viewed as evidence of his self-centredness and vileness. Why were they to come out for his burial? "What has he done for me?" Tongues started to wag. Solomon's relatives were only concerned with what they could get from the dead man. He hadn't left any will. Tani had taken away what she considered to be valuable when he died. She moved out of his house two years before he died, but had not completely severed her links with him. After all she had had two kids by him and they hadn't been formally divorced. She had just run away from him when the wind of evening had begun to threaten his eyelids. It was at that very moment the chick of her own noon started trilling. She didn't want the trilling to stop at mid-term between the vast glorious sunshine and the gloomy evening that had made his hands tremble. Who could blame her? She had her own life to live. In the final analysis, she was just a village girl who had to make good in the world. And yet fate had been able to pull a fast one on her. The chick of her noon had threatened to cease chirping just as her heart began to surge towards the fruit of her future. Solomon had stood back on the funereal threshold with a sceptre from the grave groaning under the weight of what was for her, an unbearable age. And how should she have fully appreciated what she had let herself in for? How could one have seen through the deceptive light of chandeliers, marble floors, silver cutlery, crystal and the entire glittering dream that made tomorrow such a tantalising place to peer into?

On the day of Solomon's burial, Tani wore a black veil underneath a black hat. She also donned a pair of dark sunglasses and a gown. She looked impressive to the villagers who hadn't seen such a spectacle in a long time. She didn't feel any unsupportable grief. She had turned out looking nice only to spite those whom she considered her enemies. There was a small church service and she sat in front with her children. Benu's three children also sat on the front pew while the officiating minister's voice cracked along the walls of the Baptist church.

It was almost a miracle that the burial had taken place at all. The poor relatives of the deceased wanted desperately the property and money he had left behind. He hadn't left much to their disappointment. So they turned their attention to Tani.

She's the witch that killed him. She's a greedy, selfish gold digger. Look at her fucking skin; you would hardly think she shat, said Murajade, Solomon's caustic uncle who never got on well with him. They had been debating how to inherit the shoes, clothes, wristwatches and whatnot of the dead man. Maja, another uncle of the deceased, was presiding over the family feud. He sat in the corner of the room trying to assert himself as a staunch defender of tradition. Benu was also there making a lot of noise. She was insinuating that Tani wanted to keep all the dead man's wealth to herself. Maja was not very effective but they respected him. He was the oldest. Benu's two sons sat conspicuously at opposite sides of the room looking fairly dangerous. The hatred that they felt for Tani radiated and dimmed the atmosphere. She was a bit afraid that they might try to beat her up. The morning talk dragged on into the other side of the afternoon. Tempers had risen and fallen many times before then. The dead man lay in the mortuary and his scattered brood cursed amongst themselves.

All I want to know is how my children are going to be provided for, Benu continued to say…I know he left something behind. How much, I do not know, but I'm sure if those concerned are to be fair then I wouldn't have much to worry about. Of course fair play is foreign to many people and that's why this bloody country is so backward, so underdeveloped. Even in simple family matters we can't be em..... what shall one say, democratic and yes fair-minded.

Look, Benu, are you going to allow me to arbitrate or not? All day you've been prattling and we haven't gotten anywhere.

That's because we haven't heard the truth!

Look, what truth are you going on about? said Tani, finally picking up the challenge.

I don't have to answer you. You're a small girl.

And you are an old woman, she snapped and looked at the corners of the room where Benu's children were seated. They hadn't moved from the edges of their chairs. Nonetheless they sat close to the edges, eyeing mouthy, disrespectful Tani. They would have loved to pick her up by the scruff of the neck and slapped some sense into her head. The elders in the room wouldn't permit it, but it may just as well happen. Maja sensed the tension in the air and tried to assert his authority once again.

There are few things one must learn about this life, he said. When the rich man wants to die, he goes to the back of the poor man's yard. Solomon's case is an appropriate case. Look at us here all gathered to sort out his affairs because he didn't set them straight during his lifetime.

A grave silence ensued after Tani and Benu had eyed each other viciously. Benu then got up and retied her wrap even though it hadn't been undone. Tani hissed. Maja looked at her and continued to speak.

The grasshopper and the ant were friends. The grasshopper spent his days playing and hopping about in the field during the dry season. It had not a care in the world. The bloom of wild flowers dazed by the sun was too much for it. His joy knew no bounds. He would call the ant to come and play in the fields and the ant would oblige him for a while then go back into the hole he was making against the rainy season so as to store some food. This went on for a while until the ant had secured his future. And then the rains came. Torrential, relentless and the formerly sun-dazed fields became pools and expanses of flood. The grasshopper came running to the ant's abode to seek shelter, but the ant wouldn't let him in. You can't come in here because it is too small for you, it said. Other ants and little insects continued to troop in while the grasshopper stood at the entranceway shivering and drenched with rain. All the little insects were soon in, safe and sound whilst the rain pounded on the open fields. The following morning when the ants came out, they found the grasshopper dead behind the hole. The little insects that first chanced upon him wanted to have him as a feast: he was cruel, they all cried but the ant persuaded them not to go ahead with the plan. Instead they were to give him a humane burial. And so they did. The rich man dies behind the house of the poor man. You see we ought to be careful about what we do. We should always have tomorrow in mind if not we shall just spend our lives chasing after shadows. He paused for a little while to assess the impact of his story. Other matters were looming in his mind. He too was approaching the dusk of his life and he wanted to secure some human company in the face of the inexorable hug of death. And if possible, he wanted to secure some peace for himself. He looked at Tani, but she had a scowl on her face.

We shouldn't go about chasing shadows. I shall narrate to you another parable to illustrate the point. You see the tortoise gave the chicken and the woodpecker some money to keep for a rainy day. These animals had been meeting regularly. Tortoise was the chair at the meetings and the other participants, which is to say the chicken and the woodpecker were the treasurers. At the end of one of their meetings, the chicken and the woodpecker were again given some money to keep. Do you all follow? Good. Now the woodpecker went into the woods and hid the amount given to him in a tree. The chicken on the other hand kept the amount given to him in the ground. At the subsequent meeting the woodpecker returned the amount that had been given to him for safekeeping while the chicken could not do the same. He explained that he had kept the money in the soil, but on going back to retrieve it, he couldn't find it. The animals sent him back to go and look for it again even though they suspected that the termites might have taken it away. And so till this day, the chicken continues to scratch the ground looking for the lost money. Now this particular parable teaches us two things. First and foremost, we mustn't take people at face value. You shouldn't jump to conclusions about a person's character on the basis of some superficial evidence and then two: do not spend your life chasing after shadows like a chicken.

A murmur went through the crowd. The men nodded their heads in approval, but Tani and Benu persisted in ogling one another viciously. They had other things on their minds. Maja kept giving Tani gentle looks.

It seems to me that you ladies are still angry with each other… not so? Alright, we'll tell you a little something about being angry. It is baseless, useless and unproductive. More importantly it is undignified. As he said this, he thrust his face outwards with his hands clutching firmly the armrests and looked intently at the women with widened, emphatic eyes. His light blue shirt was frayed. So were his dark grey trousers. The sandals on his feet made him look a veteran schoolmaster on a short vacation. Both women seemed to become a little calmer, but there was really no way one may have guessed what they were thinking.

Maja resumed the narration of his parables.

You see, I'd like you to know, and I mean all of you here, why anger is not only counterproductive but also empty. You see the hawk that roams about in our skies knows this very well. One day, he went to the sheep and picked up her lamb for a meal but she didn't complain. In fact she didn't even bulge so he knew something was amiss. Again one day he went to the duck and picked up one of her chicks and she too didn't complain. He didn't have to think too deeply to know that something was amiss again. But when he did the same to the chicken she made such a fuss immediately so he said to himself; she is harmless, because she's brought out what was within her. There is nothing she can do. I hope you get the point I'm making. Anger in many cases is a sign of emptiness, of powerlessness.

By the time Maja finished the narration the tales, people started to see him in a different light. He seemed very capable of handling the affairs of the family.

We have all found ourselves in these very unfortunate circumstances, but this is all part of life. What I want to assure you is that Solomon's children would not suffer... I shall see to it.

They concluded the meeting and went back to their respective homes. The bungalow Solomon had built loomed like a faded monument in its isolation. It stood in an inexplicably proud manner fighting off encroaching decay.

Oroke was agog with the news of Solomon's death, even though the villagers felt that he hadn't done anything for the improvement of his settlement. The women he left behind were also not in a position to dictate what happened in relation to the welfare of his children. Nobody was ready to bear full responsibility for these obligations and yet no one was willing to let go. Tani was still a young woman and the fact that she had two children with the dead man made her irrevocably linked to the fate of his extended family. She was supposed to spend forty days in Oroke in mourning. But the period was one in which various schemes and intrigues were concocted to see that all those remotely involved got something from the property of the dead man. No one really believed that there was nothing to be gained. Tani felt sorrowful. But the sorrow stemmed from the suffering she had endured and not from a sense of loss. Her own immediate family were not concerned about her plight. After all, she hadn't been of much help to them when the going had been good for her. She had had the luck to be married to somebody who might have proved useful in their desperate climb up the ladder of life. But she had turned her back on them and savoured all her joys of her relative good fortune alone. There is a saying that goes, he who eats alone shall die alone. She would be left to savour the bitter leaves of her labour alone just as well. So they kept away.

Tani didn't mind her circumstances. She needed every interlude of peace to be able to cope just now. She had to keep her head straight and face the harsh light ahead. She was prepared to sink in her own stew if need be. Wandu was the only one from her immediate family who had shown some kind of concern. She had come all the way to Oroke for the burial, but was staying in their family compound half a kilometre away. The compound was located behind a cluster of thickly leaved trees. A long winding path connected it to the road that led to a market. A path from the back of the compound led to the village library, which had a few old published treasures nobody bothered to read. Along these paths the grass was always about knee-high during the rainy season. The stars were usually hidden when one looked up into the skies at night because of the black canopy of leaves. And so to be expected, snakes crawled away into the unexpected reaches of the blackness looking for stray chicks and rodents. A few metres from the road, a mentally ill man called Kanida hovered underneath an almond tree. He was a big man of about six feet. He spent his days talking to the leaves and every time one fell onto the ground, his agony increased. He loved to inhale marijuana, thick jumbo-sized affairs blowing up the smoke to the birds that twittered above him. He was a notorious person. Soon he fell into serious trouble. In fact he was always falling into trouble. People tolerated him because every community needed the mentally ill; the insane were the index of how much sanity was prevailing. We need to laugh at human tragedy to obviate the profundity of our own grave shortcomings so that when we look in the faces of distressed human beings we are able to re-order the artificial categories of normalcy. But Kanida kept assaulting the established scheme of things by being able to discover new grounds of human distress.

Once, he stole a litter of puppies from a dwelling a few fields away to make his mid-day meal. It was a very sunny day but for some reason he didn't bother to return to his shelter underneath his tree. Instead he ran down a dirt road and started to assemble what he could use as cooking utensils. First of all he found himself an old and battered rusty tin, which he filled with stream water. He used a broken piece of corrugated metal as a lid and then he had made a fire right on the middle of the dirt road. He then placed all the lovely puppies in the tin. All five of them, golden, burgundy and black in the rusty tin and then he held down the rusted piece of metal which served as a lid down with his smudge-smeared palms. Soon after the water started to heat up and then he started to alternate one smudge-smeared palm with another to hold down the hot rusty lid. He cursed the fumes as the poor puppies struggled and jostled inside the tin. Those who saw him making the meal shouted at him to desist from what he was doing, but he refused to heed them. Little boys close by began to pelt with him stones from their catapults and slings. He yelled wildly each time he was struck by a missile but he still stubbornly persisted in keeping down the rusty lid. None of the boys ventured to come too close to him. They just stood at a safe distance pelting him with stones. When the puppies had died he began to tear them with his teeth. They hadn't cooked properly and blood fled from them at every bite he took and fell over his face and bare chest. He licked off the blood from the corners of his mouth and nose. The boys who were pelting him with stones got frightened and ran to their homes to report what Kanida was up to. Kanida would have a bite of fur and puppy meat and laugh wildly looking up into the centre of the scorning sun and then shake his riotous mane of hair vigorously. He was enjoying his mid-day meal.

That evening when the sun was going down for a rest, ten hefty village roughnecks paid Kanida a visit under his tree when he was having a nap. The leader of the gang struck him in the scrotum with a stick and he stirred violently.

What....what, he stammered as he looked into the faces of the young men.

I'm sure you really enjoyed yourself this afternoon. Look at his mouth, all stained with blood, said the leader poking him with the stick in his mouth. Kanida kept trying to duck as he scrambled onto his feet. He was looking for a way to escape, but he had been surrounded. The roughnecks were all armed with cudgels. Then the leader struck him hard and on the chest. He fell on the ground screaming really loudly. More cudgels fell haphazardly on him. When the tempo of the assault diminished, he would look at a particular attacker and say: I know you, you've always plotted my downfall, you've always wanted to kill me and God knows I haven't done anything to you. He knew he would soon be left alone to continue his conversations with the leaves above him. Passersby who chanced upon his plight began to plead on his behalf.

Let him alone, he was only hungry, they were saying.

You see, I told you I didn't steal the dogs, Kanida strained to interject.

You still have the mouth to talk, said the leader of the gang dealing him another blow.

He is only a madman, he means no harm.

Then he should learn to lay off the property of others.

He doesn't know anything, he is mad.

Soon afterwards he was left alone. For days his body ached badly and he was able to keep away from trouble. He smoked more joints than usual to deaden the pain. He used old discarded newspapers that had turned brown after long periods under the sun to wrap up his weed. The aroma drifted down the sun-bathed road to the huts and little grocery kiosks that stood on the other side. When he was well enough he resumed talking to the leaves. After that incident, he never went out to steal puppies again. Instead he took to stealing plantains behind a hut not too far from where he made his home. The young man who owned the plantain tree grew really puzzled by the cases of theft.

One night when he could take it no more, he hid and waited for the thief. Sure enough, Kanida stole into the yard and tore off a bunch of plantains from a tree. The man crept out of the black shadows and struck Kanida on his arms with a heavy iron rod. He slumped on to the marshy grounds and wailed continuously into the congealed silence of the night asking for help. When the man saw it was Kanida, he went into his hut to fetch a knife so he could kill him for good. Something told Kanida that he might lose his life if he didn't act fast so he found a way to get back on his feet with the help of a huge plantain leaf that drooped towards him. When the man returned with a glinting machete, Kanida was nowhere to be found. He was met by the silence, ominous, old and foreboding as the hills that surround Oroke. The darkness too had become surprisingly doubly heavy and tremulous by its pregnancies.

The following day, Kanida was seen crying beneath his tree. Farmers who were on the way to their farmsteads grew concerned.

My arms, my arms have been broken. I don't know what I did to deserve all this treatment.

When they asked him who had done it, he mentioned Kpaki, for he was the man. And he was asked why he had had his arms broken, but he would not say. So they went to see Kpaki to find out the reason. Kpaki then explained to them that Kanida had been stealing his plantains.

Is that all? asked one of the farmers.

Is it not enough? asked Kpaki.

What is the point making a mad man go through such an ordeal? asked another farmer, who was holding a particularly rusty hoe .

He is a thief!

So what? Why did you have to do such a thing to someone who is mentally ill?

I'd like to know what you would have done if it were you?

No, no, that's besides the point. The man is mad. Not normal, can't you understand?

Later on when they saw there wasn't any point arguing with Kpaki, they left him alone and went back to Kanida, where he was groaning beneath the tree. They asked him once more what had happened, but he could not explain how Kpaki had emerged from the dark shadows and had hit him with a rod on his arms. Other passersby who heard of his ordeal gave him their sympathies and promised to return with fruits. For days, Kanida's plight was the main topic of discussion in many households and drinking bars. Baskets of fruit were brought to him by sympathetic mothers. Kanida would talk about how he had been struck with a rod, but no one could make any sense of his story. But this did not stop people from seeking to find out about his ordeal. A traditional bonesetter was even assigned to mend his broken bones. After several weeks, he was healed and became once more just another village mad man. Everyone had been hoping he would die peacefully instead of always falling into harm's way. But Kanida could not help himself from falling into trouble.

One night he stole into Tani's family yard and did his worst. It was a starless moonless night and only a few fireflies beamed in the darkness embalmed scrubs and leafy undergrowths. The villagers usually opened their windows to allow fresh air to drift into their hot sweat-inducing huts. It was a humid night and there was no breeze. Everything lay humped in breathless silence. Maniyan, Tani's half-sister was sleeping in one of the rooms with her siblings. She was a quiet, passive nineteen-year-old girl. Everyone had swallowed the drug of sleep when Kanida crept through one of the windows. Before he intruded he had excreted in front of the termite eaten door.

Kanida went over the sleeping forms lying on the floor looking for breasts and other signs of womanhood. His hands found Maniyan and he lifted up his filthy loincloth. She only had a cloth over her body, which he removed and flung aside. She turned and parted her legs slightly but she was still deep in slumber. His large penis groped for her warm and sweaty crotch. A few thrusts afterwards she woke up and cried out. Her brothers, who were lying nearby, were also woken up.

What is the matter? one of them asked in throes of fright and befuddlement.

A man! A man is on top of me!

By then Kanida had risen and was fumbling towards the window through which he had ventured inside. Almost immediately one of the brothers dashed out of the door and slipped over the mound of shit just over the threshold and fell backwards, hitting his skull on the ground. Another followed suit and suffered the same fate. So they went back inside to light a couple of kerosene lamps with their feet and backs soiled with shit. Making haste, they went outside to the well behind the hut to wash away the excrement from their bodies. The naked Maniyan was claiming that the culprit had been Kanida because the man smelt exactly like him and also that he had wild bushy hair.

About four men left the yard to catch Kanida underneath his tree. They didn't find him there. It was strange because he was always there at that time of the night and it would have been senseless probing into the unyielding surroundings, cloaked as they were by the conspiratorial darkness. Kanida went on to rape three other sleeping women. And then at dawn he went and sat by the gates of the market where he thought he would be protected from his accusers. Word went round as to his whereabouts. Those who knew what he had done hissed as they passed by him. But he ignored them as he continued to gather dead leaves about himself and threw dust over his body. When the sun stood right in the middle of the skies, petrified by the energy of its own heat, a bunch of aggrieved men came for him. Kanida was really frightened. He was dragged down to the centre of the village where the hills that loomed on the northern side were visible. A large crowd had gathered to watch.

Where were you last night? they asked.

Sleeping. I'm not well. Please give me some medicine.

A club fell on his skull.

So you've left stealing for fucking women who are not yours, said Maniyan's brother.

I told you I'm not well.

The crowd was ready to tear him to pieces and it kept surging forward like hot disturbed steam. The calmer ones amongst the crowd saw the futility of mob action. It took some heavy pleading to quell the anger of the mob. The common anger wasn't completely quenched, it was only checked. Kanida had his arms firmly tied behind his back and then his legs were bent backwards and also bound to his arms. He lay completely immobile as the impersonal heat of the sun bore into his chest and ribs. Kanida gnashed his teeth incessantly while receiving kicks and blows all over the ball that his body had become. A tremendous kick caught him on his chest and his eyeballs rolled uncontrollably and then his breathing became laboured. Kanida's thorax sustained multiple fractures and he died. His corpse was dragged out of the village with a rope and deposited in a forest where evil spirits were said to make their home. Not long after, vultures came and plucked his two broken eyeballs and then started to feed on his equally broken body.

Tạni visited her family compound to commiserate with her half sister.

This is such a vile place. All kinds of things happen here. I just want to leave. Imagine this kind of thing. It's so disgraceful, tragic.

Maniyan was sobbing. A few relatives were sitting around in the virtually bare parlour.

This isn't a matter of tears. Anyway the bastard has been killed. It serves him right. I have to take you to the clinic to make sure you haven't contracted any disease. Imagine being fucked by a mad man. And all those public tongues would be wagging, those bloody hypocrites! I can't believe it. I just hope you don't get pregnant.

God forbid! snapped some of the relatives who had gathered around.

But just imagine what had happened. It's an abomination, volunteered another.

Would you all shut up? said Tani. You are the very ones who would start to go from one bar to another laughing at the poor girl. Mind you, I know who my enemies are!

Heaven forbid, said the one who had spoken first. May I be stricken by thunder if I do any such thing.

Well, thank you for your concern. You may now all leave, Tani said, standing by the door. They all filed out, walking gingerly as if they were within the confines of a shrine.

Tani's eyes were avoided. Her body stood erect by the doorway. When they got out of earshot, they started to laugh as they headed for a drinking bar.

Weeks passed and it was found out that Maniyan wasn't pregnant. She was also certified healthy. But when she went out, the men she had ditched pointed mordant fingers at her. For some time, Oroke knew some peace. Tani continued to avoid forming strong ties with anyone in the village. She had come back only because Solomon was dead and some family matters needed to be sorted out. She had really come a long way. She who had started off by hawking pepper, bread and kolanuts with dust all over her on hidden paths had been able to go to the city to be smitten by its exotic lights, its innumerable modern attractions. Oroke was now so small and constricting. Who would have thought she would get to where she was today? Who would have thought she would be able to escape a place where one wore rags from cradle to grave? Who would have thought... Well, that was what life was about. The treasures and surprises in the various recesses of tomorrow were simply unpredictable. She had always reminded herself not to let her gaze stray from the next bright spell of sunshine. Dusk was only a camouflage, a deception ranged against hidden laughter. Her soul had always hungered for that reign of laughter that she believed Oroke couldn't give her. When the forests spoke to her, their depths revealed an arboraceous prison house against which she fought with all her might. So thin and frail was she then, but her determination was absolute. She had been resolute to escape the life of dust and dirt that fate sought to impose upon her. She had to hear her voice breaking against the waves of the ocean down south.

Tani had been a rebellious teenager. When her mother sent her to the village stream to fetch water, she often went off to play with a group of boys much younger than her. Their ages ranged between ten and fourteen. There was a clearing at the mouth of the stream where they played. Tani the queen sat in the middle of the five or six boys who sang and danced for her. They called her mother. She would later divest them of their shorts to fiddle with their small taut members. She then undid her wrap and spread her legs while she stroked her vagina with their ticklish members. They took turns to mount her and then jumped off when it got too ticklish. They didn't fully understand the games they played but they thoroughly enjoyed them. Soon every little boy in the village wanted to come with Tani to the stream. They loved to run their fingers up her thighs and up to her small firm breasts and watch her when the sensations made her jerk. The boys jumped over her from one side to the other singing or screaming. She made them happy. Their games went on for about a year.

A year later, Kogbura, one of the boys, came to understand fully the games they played. He had turned fifteen. Kogbura would send other boys up the trees to sing like birds so that they wouldn't forget the songs that grew out of the bowels of their soil. They all wanted to go into the cities, to ride in big motorcars and watch the night descend into the amber lights of the skyscrapers. They had to sing those songs across the skies so that they wouldn't forget them.

When they had gone up the trees, Kogbura would come on top of Tani and make love like a full grown man. The songs rang out of the leaves until some voices fell hoarse. Then they would come down and Kogbura would ask them who told them to and send them up the trees again after knocking their heads together and whipping them with a cane. They feared him enormously. He was not only stronger than them all, but he was also the smartest.

Kogbura took to sending the pack of boys on errands. He instructed them to take a step and count up to five before they took the next one. They took ages in coming back and no one attempted to disobey him. He could get very vicious. Once they were all away, Kogbura would make love to Tani like a man. He kept shouting after them, the first brat to return would be beaten up. When they finally returned and wanted to resume their games of nakedness with Tani, she would not allow them because Kogbura had told her so. Some of the boys reported the matter to their parents at home. Word went from one angry mouth to another saying Tani had been raping the boys. She was severely reprimanded and told to desist from corrupting the boys. The boys on their part did not want to stop trailing her around.

Later, she started an affair with a man who owned a small provision store. His name was Lakun. He spent his days in his virtually bare store trying to find something to do with himself. The boys would be offered a sweet each and sometimes they are instructed to shave off the hair in his armpits. Afterwards they were sent out to play. Lakun would make love to Tani all afternoon until towards dusk when the boys returned to fetch her. They were then offered another round of sweets and sent away.

Tani enjoyed fucking. Everyone in the village came to know this about her. Not long after, Tani was sitting on a bench at the back of the hut and playing with a knife, which she held between her legs. She had been asked to peel some yams by her mother. The pack of boys that trailed after her were playing around the compound. Tani was singing and cutting through the air within her thighs until she cut herself just beside the clitoris. She dropped the knife leapt on her feet and screamed when she saw blood spurting out her. What is the matter? her mother asked, rushing out of the house. She had her hands over her bosom and then when she saw what had happened she too screamed and then lifted her hands upon her head.

Quick, go and get me the native doctor who lives near the market. Go now! And tell him it is a matter of life and death, she shouted at the boys who started to run off immediately. The native doctor, a thin man of about fifty-five, was soon on his way. He met Tani's mother stamping her feet and doing up and undoing the wrap meant for her body. Tani was saying, I am dead, I am dead, I am dead.

Shut up, he snapped at her, let me see what you have done to yourself. She opened her legs for him to see the cut. Her pubic hair was covered with blood, as was the bench on which she sat. The doctor brought out a razor and began to shave off her pubic hair and then he dabbed the cut with a rag to reduce the bleeding. He went on to stitch up the wound. Before that, he put a finger into Tani's vagina and asked her if she had been with a man that day.

No, she cried. He put his hand into her vagina again and showed Tani's mother a globule of semen. And she says she hasn't been near a man today. He shook his head. Her mother couldn't be bothered whether she had just fucked someone or not. She only wanted her daughter's life saved. The boys who followed her everywhere laughed at her until they were driven away by her mother. Although her mother had stood by her, Tani didn't love her. The feeling was basically mutual, but they had to keep appearances. In time, the wound healed.

After all, that was what really mattered. Her mother too had the tales of her life to tell just as everyone else. Some get lost in the hazy rivulets of the soul and others stick to the surface like the hell chamber of private suns, burning holes, huge ugly holes into the backside of human dreams and pulsating hours. Life is full of those terrible bruises that latch onto memory like leeches sucking relentlessly at the fluids of existence and dignity. Those bruises that want to make one return to the womb and start all over again, that make one want to turn away from light and remain in primal darkness forever. Foolish acts that repeatedly butt into spaces of disgrace, so that every time one remembers a deed of folly, one just hopelessly wishes the cracked looking glass of the soul would miraculously reassemble itself afresh from the debris. But hope is futile against those gnawing bouts of shame.

Tani's mother had been forced to marry an old man against her wish when she had been still very young. She never allowed the old man to lay a hand on her even though they slept on the same bed. She felt ashamed that she hadn't run away, far off with her true love, who had been waiting for her. And so every night before she went to bed, she tied her legs together with a rope so that the old man wouldn't be able to make love to her.

You are my wife, he would say to her. Why do you torment me like this? Don't you know God doesn't condone this kind of thing?

Get lost, you dirty old man.

I am your husband, Faka.

Whose husband? Please don't say that again.

What shall I say then?

Say anything you like but just know that I am not your wife.

Faka, can't you stop tormenting me?

Look, Digba or whatever your name is, would you just leave me alone in peace and allow me to sleep?

But can't you see that I love you, Faka?

He would then attempt to fondle her thighs and she'd scream: Come out neighbours! Come out! Help, help, help!

Their neighbours would come running to their hut. A few bold ones would venture into it and then see the old man who would then begin to placate them. It happened quite a few times, but he didn't allow her to leave him. It was only after she had told him that she had mixed shit into his food and given it to him to eat that she was able to take her leave of him.

Faka didn't look back. She ran off to the next village where her true love was waiting. They married even though it was not sanctioned by their families. But it didn't matter. What was important was that they were together. Their first three children were born and then her man went to town chasing skirt and drinking heavily. There was no one Faka could report him to because nobody had approved of their marriage in the first place.

You're not going out tonight, she told him once as he picked up his wine gourd to go out for yet another drinking spree.

Are you out of your mind?

You're the one who has a screw loose.

Get your paws off my jumper.

You would have to walk over me this night.

I will, he yelled and then gave her a punch on the face. She fell onto the floor and he stepped over her into the darkness.

She decided it was no good trying to get him to change his ways through words. She thought it best to start conducting her own extramarital affairs. It was easy because men were easily drawn to her. On market days she would garnish herself and walk seductively all over the village. The men understood her tactic of attraction, but she ensured that she didn't fall for the first available man. On one of such days, she walked pass a couple of wine bars and the men who sat out drinking whistled after her amid the dust and blazing sunshine. And then one of them got up and followed.

Excuse me, he said, I'd like to have a word with you.

What about?

I've been watching you for a very long time and ...

Well, speak up, aren't you a man?

I like you ...

You like what?

I said I like you.

So you like me… A sneer appeared in her face. The man's drinking companions had gathered within earshot at the mud and wood doorway that led inside the bar to know first-hand how events would unfold. Faka looked at them disdainfully and then turned to her interlocutor:

So you like me.

Well, yes, I told you.

You really like me.

The man nodded for the umpteenth time.

But have you taken a good look at yourself?

Why?

You should know exactly how ugly you are.

His friends burst out laughing.

Really, the embarrassed man said.

It's surprising that you this ugly man, really ugly, if you know what I mean should take a fancy for beautiful things.

With this, she sauntered away in the midst of a din of derisive laughter. The jilted man really got offended. He could not bear the taunting of his friends and in that hideously banal way, he felt small, reduced to the space reserved for laughingstocks. And so he plotted to have Faka poisoned. He wanted her dead at any cost. It didn't really matter how he did it, but he thought death by poisoning would be the least complicated approach. For weeks he schemed but he didn't get the kind of opportunity he wanted. Then his bitterness began to subside. The desire to have her dead subsequently wore off. But he had nurtured the germ of evil intent in his mind and it had to be destroyed as custom demanded. He had to be sanctified so that whatever balance existed in his life before, would be restored. He needed to neutralise the toxins in his heart. He hadn't also read Faka's true intentions well. Faka would not have minded having him at all. She just did not want to appear too available, in stark language, too cheap.

A few days later when it was midnight, he went to Faka's backyard as custom required in order to expunge the seed of evil intent from the pit of his stomach. Faka's family was already asleep, including Faka herself. Bariba, the man carrying out the midnight rite danced with his wrap hitched above his bare buttocks around the backyard. Alone, he sang, with a grave and contrite voice. He danced around the dark backyard thrusting his buttocks around the area where the compound well was located. He gyrated past the well and reached the edges of the little goat pen and chicken coop like a sedated baboon.

After the midnight ritual, Faka forgave him and probably forgot about all that had transpired between them. She had other things in her mind. Her husband went about the village skirt chasing and she needed to teach him a lesson. She began to go after every man for whom she took a liking. News drifted back to her husband about her escapades.

I hear you open your legs for just any man, even without being asked. Are you so cheap?

Whom are you talking to?

You whore.

Oh, I see you're feeling hurt but never remembered that what is good for the goose is also good for the gander.

You had better stop dragging my name in the mud.

You have no name worth having! You fool.

I won't hit you but remember that I've warned you.

There's nothing you can do to me.

Okay, we shall see.

He went into the bedroom and didn't utter another word. Faka, on the other hand fumed all day long. News of his wife's extramarital activities continued to drift into his ears in places where men gathered to drink and swap stories. When urged to comment on the rumours, he merely smiled through the froth of his wine and assured his friends everything was alright. All was certainly alright until the night the entire neighbourhood was woken up by the piercing racket of Faka's screaming.

Help, he wants to kill me, help help help.

Since Faka was considered notorious by the village community, people were slow in turning up. Faka had stopped her wild wailing but she was still weeping and whimpering. Her husband was seen washing his left arm in a basin in front of the house. The puzzled neighbours asked him about what had transpired between him and his wife and he directed them inside to the room where his wife was crying. Once most of them had entered, he walked out of the compound and disappeared into the night.

What happened? they asked.

Faka had her legs spread out and was clutching her abdomen and her loins.

He put his fist into my womb.

Oh poor dear, said an elderly woman. Oh dear, how cruel of him. Can you believe that? Men! They are such awful devils. Don't worry, I will get you some herbs that would soothe you at the crack of dawn.

A man standing by the elderly woman then told the gathering:

She must have done something really bad to her husband ... ask her what she's done!

Not in this condition. She can hardly talk.

Women are the devils.

Men are the demons, said a young wife.

I said we ought to find out what she did to him, said the man.

Oh, it must be the usual stuff, said another man.

These women are real devils.

That is a lie and even then you can't do without us.

Faka continued to cry until it was morning. The elderly woman went into the bushes when the first glimmer of light beamed through the skies and brought back the herbs.

****

Faka, Tani's mother died some years later, but she wasn't missed. Instead, Tani was full of self-pity because she felt her life was full of sorrow. She hadn't known a mother's love nor a father's. She had just wanted to run away from home. Her own marriage had been a failure. She had no friends she could trust. And now her husband was dead. She felt so alone and so sought help from one of her aunts, a woman who had known true sorrow, but because she hid it well and was always cheerful, people confided in her.

Aunty, I feel my life is a disaster, no formal schooling, a shattered marriage and now my husband is dead. And I might go back to a living death of squalor and wretchedness.

Alright child, I'll take you to a man, a fortune teller of some sort who might be able to help you tomorrow at dusk.

Please anything to help me. My bitterness is too much for me.

The man Tani was taken to was short, with a disagreeable set of teeth. His eyes glinted eagerly, but he hardly looked intelligent. Instead, he seemed to be an unfortunate crook.

What's the problem? he asked brusquely.

I'm so sad.

How sad? Because we all get sad sometimes.

Very sad. In fact, I feel I'm the saddest woman in the world.

Really? That's a very serious allegation. Alright, you know what you can do for me?

What?

I shall send you on an errand. It can take you to any corner of the world.

Please say it.

I want you to bring back a handful of soil from the compound of any family that hasn't experienced death in this life.

Tani suddenly realised how foolish she had been. Instead she knew the futility of the errand he was sending her so she gave him some money, thanked him and left with her aunt for home. What a fool she had been, she thought. She remembered her father who probably had a more tragic life than herself. He had slept one night in his hut with only a wrapper over his body. He possessed a lot of cats, which he kept to keep rats away. During the course of a night, his wrap slipped from his body onto the ground. He was lying on his back. A cat that saw his throbbing member, leapt across the dark and thrust its fangs into it. Blood sprouted into the night. Tears, cries, frantic tossing. Too late. He wasn't able to use his member again even though it was stitched back on. We all carry our crosses to the grave one way or the other.

Life is full of those irrevocable, irreparable cesspools of sorrow that the heart and mouth can never find ways to utter truthfully and completely. Tani went more often to her family compound now to stop herself from thinking too much. Sometimes she even slept there. Expectedly, members of the extended family became very pleased with her. During the evenings, she loved to sit on a stool beneath the baobab tree that stood to the left side of the compound. A monkey that was owned by the family swung from tree to tree, chattering. The kids in the compound used to chase it about and it chased them back in return. Neni, Tani's cousin's four-year-old daughter was always falling victim to the monkey. When she sat under the baobab tree alone eating a meal, it would come and scratch her back to distract her and then run off with her dish and then she would burst out sobbing. The adults who were within the compound would run after the thieving monkey. They almost never caught up with it. Sukuman loved to chase after the mischievous monkey. He and his sister had been staying with Maja. However, the monkey had to be killed when it was caught fondling Neni's private parts. This greatly saddened the children of the compound. But it was the least of Tani's worries. In fact, she supported the killing of the monkey.

As dusk approached, she remembered the beauty contest in which she had met Solomon. She recalled the frantic preparations they all made to see to the success of the show. Every girl wanted to compete and win the cash prize and electronic gadgets that went along with it. She remembered the vast community hall in which it was held, the night party that followed, dancing in front of the live band that played traditional music, even the poorly painted white walls of the hall. They hadn't even painted the exterior of the building. She went in and out of it full of false pride in herself. Bright lipstick and cheap perfume, a glittering gown, black with yellow spots studded with rhinestones. The jealousy and mutual envy that bit into the lips of contestants. Solomon was seated at the high table with other guests. It had been a long table that took almost the entire breadth of the hall, even though there hadn't been many guests seated behind it. The few bottles of low-grade wine, saucers of fried beef and jollof on a white gleaming tablecloth that had been purchased from the village market impressed the expectant villagers. Dirty kids kept leaping in and out through the glassless windows only to be beaten back by village toughs who were brandishing whistling whips made from sheep hide. The live band of indifferent calibre sang old popular highlife tunes.

How she had danced on that night. That was the night on which she trapped Solomon inside the pools of her eyes. The pools led to an unquenchable hunger of the heart and threw her into the whirlpool at the mouth of the world, so she tried to get out of the world's whirlpool through the greying hairs of Solomon. She had thought he kept bright crystals in his belly so that when she came into their illuminating range, the hunger of her heart, her life would evaporate as fast as a fleeing bird. Birds of joy had dropped out of the sky like black mysterious ribbons. A hall full of young virile men in extravagant gowns beckoned. The dazzling gowns flowed impersonally over the penury of hardened bodies so that when the men rose up again the following day biting chewing sticks, the black, glistening, muscled bodies caught the light of dawn like a challenge. Most of them had danced ripples out of their bodies. They had endured almost endless waves of motion over pools of sweat. The contestants of the beauty contest danced too as if that was what they needed to do to win. And really dancing well was an added advantage. It was a night filled with moist hot loins, soaked armpits, drenched underwear and bras. And yet there had been no cool drinks around.

The rounds of distanced drumming crashed through the drowsy rhythms of the sunset. Tani strained her ears to know what was going on. Minutes later, the drum beats and shouting drifted up towards her.

Lodan
Thief thief thief
Lodan
Thief thief thief

Wait a minute. Wasn't Lodan the girl she had known as a child?

The one who had the noticeable look of a tragic orphan?

Cassava is gone
Thief thief thief
The yams have gone
Thief thief thief
The plaintain too
Thief thief thief

The kids in the compound leapt towards the road that led to the noise, trailed by the adults. Tani remained by the roadside waiting. She wanted to find out if it was the Lodan she knew. The crowd emerged from the last incline of the road led by the Lord of the Brats. He was in charge of dealing with cases involving theft. It was the Lodan she knew. There were yams, cassava and plantains in the basket that stood on her head. She was naked and tears were streaming down her face. Tani rushed up to meet the crowd, but she was repelled from venturing into the confusion of the mob. There was nothing she could do anyway. Lodan, she later learnt, had been caught stealing on a farm. She was then tried and found guilty. The next step was inflicting punishment. She was taken round the village with a crowd of people taunting her. White marks of shame had been drawn all over her face and her body. They took her around, singing. They jeered at her. They took her from compound to compound and took back her name. And when that happens one might as well be dead. She would spend the remainder of her days on the fringes of everything; light, song, laughter, dusk, community and even death. She would be locked out of conversation and would stay on the edges of the village like a forever stranded and dying shadow. She wouldn't even have the courage to flutter on those forlorn edges. She would dig into the hard ground alone, chewing the hard and bitter yield. Rags would eat into the soreness of her body, but would not grant her the wisdom they bestow on the wise and aged. She could expect her womb to turn and shrivel until she is flung into a small sandy grave. Her name would be bled until it became a bloodless relic to be tossed about periodically in vile village conversations. Then life would have been snatched from her, she would wear the dust of her burial before her actual death. Acts of theft in the village had profound symbolic meanings. They meant a destruction of the communal bond, a deep psychosocial disturbance, a severance at the heart of community, an injury to peace and truth. Acts of theft were tantamount to both madness and death. Lodan was taken to a shrine. The chief priest had been waiting. She kept her hands over her shaved genitals. The drumming and singing subsided.

So this is the thief, said the priest.

Yes, said the Lord of the Brats.

This is the woman who is trying to soil the name of our village. Right? Then in that case, we shall take back the name we have given you now. You don't deserve it.

Lodan stood in a corner whimpering. From time to time she was pushed towards the centre of the shrine. The chief priest was preparing a concoction she was to drink. When he finished, he poured out some of the liquid into a small calabash and said:

You see, this drink is a drink that gods use as a snare. If ever you steal anything again, you shall die immediately. Like I have said, it is a noose that gods put around the necks of those with itchy fingers.

He then placed the calabash before a wall on which many talismanic objects hung. Lodan was still shaking and whimpering. The men poked her with clubs and sticks towards the drink. When she got to it, she bent down to pick it up. A couple of men behind her put sticks through her loins. She jumped in fright and the crowd burst out laughing. She tried to pick it up again and the same thing happened. More laughter emerged from the crowd. When she attempted to pick it up for the third time, she kept looking over her trembling shoulder like a frightened dog. Jerkily, she drank the contents of the calabash and then she was taken to the police station where a complaint was lodged. That was the end of her as a part of the community; a perpetual blemish had swamped her family name. Her children would be pointed at as they walked through the village paths. No one would ever play with them with innocence in their hearts.

In Tani's family yard that evening, a meal of duck, spinach and melon soup was being prepared. The live duck was held upside down and tied to a cord. The bird started to flap its wings continuously. Soon it began to vomit all sorts of things; rotten papaw remains, millipedes, centipedes, earthworms, strings, cockroaches, seeds from wild fruit, and little pebbles. It went on flapping its wings for hours and then it was untied and brought down by a woman who was part of the family. She took it to a corner in the yard and dug a hole in the ground to gather duck blood. A rough looking knife was held to its neck. She uttered a few silent words of prayer and slaughtered the exhausted bird. The impaled bird jerked and struggled vainly within the shadow of death. After the final jerk, its warm blood lay still, its body, stone dead. It was thrown into a cauldron of hot water. A couple of other women made fire with wood and chattered endlessly as they plucked feathers. Yams were peeled and thrown into a pot that sat over a fire. That night, the entire family had pounded yam, melon soup and duck for dinner.

The following evening, Tani's uncle Jeremiah said he enjoyed the meal of the previous night so much that he wanted something just as good again. He was a practicing member of a cult that relished eating dog meat and he thought it wouldn't be such a bad idea if they had some for the evening meal. His cult made all kinds of delicacies with dog; grilled peppered dog, dog meat pepper soup, dog with assorted vegetables and dog with palm wine. Tani protested, but it didn't make any difference. Moko, a fine looking brown dog was chosen by Jeremiah, who set three young men who were also his sons to go after him. A bowl of bones was put in front of Moko who started to sniff and gnaw at them joyously. Two of the young men held iron rods behind their backs. Moko went on devouring the bones. When the other dogs wanted to join him, they were driven away. Just as Moko became totally oblivious of his surroundings, he was struck very violently on the skull. It had to be done only once, he slumped on all fours and a deathlike eclipse started to slide down his pale eyes. Another man quickly brought out a knife. Moko's death throes weren't violent and he was slaughtered without much fuss. All the other dogs in the yard started to bark and howl from a distance. They barked and howled continuously over the death of Moko. Later, when Moko's bones were thrown at them, they fought over them.

This dog meat is so greasy, Jeremiah complained as he sank his teeth into dog flesh. Who cooked it?

Lekpan, said a woman who had brought him a bowl of water.

Lekpan! he shouted.

A worn-out woman appeared gliding like a broken feather over the threshold of his hut.

You made this? he asked, pointing at a sizeable portion of dog meat.

Yes, sir.

Don't you know how to make it?

I did my best, sir.

Well, your best is very poor, he said and wiped off the oil that was dripping out of the corners of his mouth.

I will try harder next time.

When you want to make a dish of dog, you must always remember to avoid putting too much cooking oil in the pot because the meat itself is very oily.

Yes, sir.

You can go now.

Yes, sir. Thank you, sir.

Jeremiah resumed eating his meal of dog. Most of the women in the yard refused to eat. The little girls did as their mothers in not eating, but the boys laughed and relished their meals of dog. The women kept all the utensils that had been used in preparing dog aside and never used them again. Jeremiah would offer his friends who cared for it some fried piece of dog, which they had with calabashes of palm wine.

There is nothing as appetising, as tasteful as dog downed with palm wine, he would say.

No, not true, wait until you've had this stuff with a bowl of garri soaked in cool stream water, said his friend Lakori.

You don't say.

Look, one of these days I shall invite you over to my place and give you the delicious stuff. I took Bendima to my place one day and gave him the stuff. You know ordinarily, he would not touch dog, but it was so good he started to come begging to have the stuff with garri at every given opportunity.

It's fabulous, you just wait and see.

Why do you men continue to do ungodly things? Tani asked as she came inside.

Do you mean eating dog is ungodly? asked Lakori.

Of course it is.

Leave her alone, she doesn't know anything about this matter, she doesn't know it is blasphemous to talk that way. Nor does she know that the ways of God instruct us to kill and eat, Jeremiah said.

I know it is terribly paganistic.

Paganistic? Lakori sneered looking at his friend.

I said don't mind her, she is just a little girl.

I'm not a little girl, I have two children and I know these kinds of practices should stop. After all, we are not animals.

Who told you that eating dog makes one a barbarian? Jeremiah asked with yet another menacing sneer.

I didn't call you a barbarian.

Well, that's what you've just said, isn't that so, Lakori?

That is what I seem to have heard.

I didn't call you a barbarian. I am only trying to point out that it has become paganistic to eat dog meat.

You young folks don't know what you are missing in the name of your so-called Christian civilisation, Lakori said.

I pity them.

Too much.

You're the ones to be pitied.

Look, we've lived like our forefathers lived their lives. We've been faithful to our tradition and culture. You are the lost one because you are neither here nor there. You are all a bunch of lost children looking for an anchor you'll never find until you return to the ways of our fathers, Jeremiah said.

Yes, that's very correct, so what do you have to say?

I hope you will see the light soon, said Tani folding her arms over her bosom.

Who wants to see your hideous light, snapped Jeremiah.

I wonder, said his friend.

The light of our fathers has kept us all very safe-- I don't know about you.

Tani, knowing that it was impossible to convince the two, bade them goodnight and took her leave. From her room, she heard them chatting far into the night. The following morning, she tipped some of the women in the compound to scrub the pots, pans and dishes thoroughly with soil and instructed them to keep them reserved separately for dog.

Two weeks later, Jeremiah said he wanted a meal of cat.

Why don't you stick to eating goat and chicken? Tani asked in frustration.

It's boring eating the same thing all the time.

So that's why we must eat poison?

Who told you that cat is poison?

They are such horrid animals to eat.

Look, all I know is that they taste lovely.

Lovely? That is hardly true.

I will give you some today.

God forbid.

Well, we have nothing to argue about.

You should at least think of the children and the purpose that cats serve in chasing away rats.

Nothing will go wrong. I've eaten cat all my life and nothing ever went wrong.

There was no point arguing so Tani left him.

Jeremiah called his first and second sons and asked them to slaughter a cat for him. They didn't like the errand, but there was nothing they could do. The chickens in the yard kept pecking away. The dogs lay in the shade sleeping. Lizards clung to tree trunks and the few cats that could be seen found a comfortable corner within the hut in which to lie. The first son got a maize sack and lured one of the cats inside. He then took it to the back of the yard where he was certain the other cats wouldn't see him. Manari, the second son who was also a schoolteacher, struck the bulge within the sack but missed it. The cat leapt within the sack and came up as high as his face. He struck again when it had settled and this time he struck the bulge right at the middle. The bulge collapsed a little, but continued twitching and tossing. He took the knife, which he had with him, to open up the dead cat's throat. Its warm blood flowed into the hole he had dug. It wasn't much. He began to skin the dead animal after he had soaked it in a basin filled with hot water. Tani stood afar watching in disgust. They paid her no attention. Jeremiah came round to see how they were getting along. A fresh pot of soup was made with the animal and the three men had some garri to go with it.

Jeremiah ate human beings. Everyone knew that, since he never bothered to hide it. He would go with a few men to the outskirts of the village to accost anybody who had the misfortune of stumbling into his way. A friend had asked him why he found eating human beings agreeable.

Look at a goat. It doesn't eat salt, pepper, onion, tomatoes, oil and those other things, yet it's so delicious. We human beings that eat all those other things are.... what shall I say, immeasurable in connection with what we are talking about.

Is that so? his friend asked.

Yeah, what do you think?

The last time he went after a human being, he chose the wrong person. The man was found wandering in a ruined farmstead, talking to himself. He was clearly losing his mind. Jeremiah killed the man and ate him together with his lungs, heart and brain. His tongue and genitals were devoured too. Years after, Koribo, Jeremiah's son became insane. He was taken to the hovel of an herbalist, where he was tied, hands and feet. The herbalist had attributed his illness to his father's past misdeeds, the killing and eating of a man who was mentally ill. Koribo got better after a few days and was released. On the night he was released, he found himself a machete with which he went prowling around. People were lying outside their huts because of the immense heat. A pale moon hung out of the expansive greyish darkness. There weren't too many mosquitoes and people were able to sleep soundly. Koribo went over to sleeping families, dealing them deadly machete cuts. Nine people were killed and several were maimed. People sustained cuts over their noses, across the eyes, and on their foreheads. A pregnant woman lost her life and unborn child. The tragedy occurred within an hour. By dawn, a search party had been organised to apprehend Koribo. He was found on top of a garbage heap, scavenging for food. They caught him and tied his hands and feet together, behind his back, just as they had done to Kanida. Karibo shrieked all the way as they carried him to the village square. They didn't have to beat him. The pain inflicted upon him sufficed. He shrieked to his death. His victims who survived went about carrying ugly scars on their faces. Nothing could be done for them. Manari found a place and moved out of the family yard after the death of his brother. He was angry with his father and nobody was able to stop him from leaving. And he also got himself a wife without the consent of his old man. She went out at dawn to do farm work while he went to the village school. He taught mathematics in the school and all the children feared him because he did not spare the rod for any misdemeanour. And then he faced a problem. Each time he went to work and his wife left the hut, a thief would come and steal his foodstuffs. He talked to a few friends about the matter, but no one came up with a solution. The only clue he found was the garri grains he saw leading up to the huge mango tree that stood in his backyard. He looked up at the tree and found no one there.

He showed his wife the trail of garri and devised a plan to catch the culprit. She was to go to the farm soon after he left the following morning. He would then make a detour and head for some bushes nearby where he could see the mango tree. On the appointed morning, he saw a boy of about ten years of age climb up the mango tree where the surrounding plains could be scanned for miles. The boy waited for several minutes. It seemed as if his eyes were fixed on his kitchen window.

Manari couched by his old bicycle watching. The boy started to descend through the branches of the fruitless tree. He looked stealthily around him and stole towards the kitchen door. He then unhinged the weak door and found the kitchen quite empty. A pot of soup lay on a board by a kerosene stove. By a corner of the kitchen, there was a little store where bags of garri, beans and some tubers of cocoyam were kept. The pot of soup was placed on the charcoal scarred floor and he scooped out a chunk of meat, which he chewed greedily. Just as he picked up a second chunk, the kitchen door was flung open. Manari barged in with a wicked sneer on his face.

So, you are the thief?

Please sir, said the boy attempting to get up.

Please? This isn't a matter of begging! I've caught you today and I'll make sure you don't ever steal again.

Please, sir, said the boy, his hands together in supplication and his lips pouting miserably.

Shut up! said Manari striking him across the face. The boy fell to the floor and his face got smeared with charcoal. The torn seat of his shorts also got smeared with black smudge.

Get up, you little bastard! I'll show you not to steal again, get up, I say!

He held the boy by the collar of his shirt and took him to the outer room that served as a sitting area.

Did you enjoy the soup?

The boy stood silent, trembling while Manari laughed at his own joke alone. His laughter pierced the haunting silence of the afternoon. The heart of the boy was beating randomly as shivers of fright tore through his young body. His hands trembled before him as sweat broke out all over him.

Please, sir, he said again.

I say, don't beg me you little bastard! Manari yelled, striking him on the face again. The nearest hut was a couple of kilometres away and no one was likely to come around. And so it was no use shouting for help.

The sun was hidden because of the dirty curtains that hung over the dusty wooden windows and frames. The bare floor looked forsaken, scattered maps of cement and mud. Outside, a breeze drifted into the mango tree and its leaves hissed and switched as if they were approving something. A painful feeling of imperfection, of inadequacy clung to the boy's throat and reels from his short life flitted through the back of his eyes like skewered images from a broken camera. Voices thundered upon him, voices urging caution and righteousness that he had never paid much attention to, reverberated against the tremulous cords of his fleeing heart. Urgent intimations of end time bled out of his young heart.

Now, you little bastard, you have three options. One, would you like me to cut out your two eyes with a razor or would you like me to break both of your legs or would your like me to cut off one of your ears? Speak out fast-- I have no time to waste.

The voices and images flitting through the boy's mind drifted on even faster.

The harsh glare of sunlight beamed ever more brightly on the proceedings.

My ear, sir, said the boy with a voice drained by fear.

You would like me to cut off your ear?

Yes, sir.

Well good, at least we're getting somewhere.

He dragged the boy by both hands to a wooden box at the other end of the room. Inside, he found a new packet of razor blades. The boy's skin tingled. An ominous shade stood at the centre of the room. Holding onto the boy with one hand, he managed to fish out a clean blade. The boy attempted to beg once more, but he realised that there was no point. It seemed as if his heart stood out on the edges of his chest waiting to bolt, anywhere, for instance, into a cool brook where the chirping of birds overhead could soothe the whole of his fear stricken being.

Shut your eyes, said Manari.

The boy did as he had been told, but quickly opened them again through an involuntary act of fear.

He shut his eyes tightly in a way that made the muscles around them hurt.

Shut your eyes, I said.

He saw blood from his ear jumping over the mango tree in the background. It was the blood that was meant to gush out of the side of his head. Fear completely overtook him, so he opened them again. Then he shut them once more. Images raced through his tortured brain and then crashed into the blackness that was tormenting his eyes.

Shut your eyes, damn it.

There was an old sheet of newspaper on the box. The razor blade shone brightly in Manari's fingers. An old sweaty smell rose through the rooms of the hut and hit the boy's nostrils. Manari was used to it.

Aaaaaaaaaaaaaaaah! shrieked the boy.

The ominous shade of silence that had tightened around the room snapped like a dry, dead twig. Blood in the afternoon. Blood in the desolate yard. Blood leaping through the brain.

Blood across the branches of the mango trees into the shades. Blood glinting inside the darkness behind the eyes. Blood further ruining the lens of an already broken camera. In the yard, the view from the top of the mango tree seemed to be calling out to all the nooks and crannies of Oroke.

Aaaaaaaaaaaaaaaah! cried the boy again.

He held both of his palms against the wound. Blood dripped quickly out of his fingers. His mouth was opened. Delayed but growing pain coursed through his young body and folded him into two on the filthy floor.

That would teach you not to steal again.

Manari took the severed ear and placed it on the old sheet of newspaper that was fluttering on the box. When the boy saw the severed ear twitching, he shat and pissed in his shorts at the same time. Manari struck him on the skull and hissed. He was going to preserve the ear for his children, to show them how he had dealt with a thief that had given him so much cause for worry. By now the dirty white school shirt the boy was wearing had become thoroughly soaked with blood.

Get out of here fast and don't let me see you here again!

Yes, sir, cried the boy through a flood of tears and blood. He bent forward and turned to go through the kitchen door.

No! go through the front door, bastard.

Yes, sir, he cried again and bent over forward, running through a shower of blood. Beads of sweat stood out on his forehead. Manari was angry that the floor had become stained with blood. He stood by the entranceway watching the progress of the boy.

Serves him right, he kept muttering to himself. He watched until the dejected pain laden form vanished from view behind the trees and hillocks. He wiped the blood from his hands with a rag and threw the blade out of the window. The ear had stained the newspaper sheet. He picked up the ear and washed out the blood inside a small basin of stream water. Then he placed it on the rusty corrugated sheet above the chicken coop to dry. For days, he would sprinkle generous amounts of salt over it.

The following morning, a contingent of village elders came to find out what had happened. Manari wasn't in the mood to receive visitors.

Why don't you find out from the boy? he retorted.

Well, we have and from what we can gather, it was only a minor thing.

A minor thing? You call kleptomania a minor thing? I can see you're a bunch of jokers. Look, I have better things to do.

We said nothing like that, we are merely reporting to you what the boy told us.

The boy is a liar! He stole repeatedly from me and I had to deal with him the hard way.

We all know that our village frowns upon stealing. We know that our ancestors forbid it. But we also have our ways of handling such matters. After all, what is the law for?

Then where were you all when the motherfucker kept on doing damage to my barn? Where were you? And now you come here to bother me with your useless questions.

Did I hear you say useless? grimaced a bald old man.

What cheek, said another.

Look if you haven't got anything more to say, I'll have to leave you. I've got work to do.

I think we have to report this matter to the police. The police will be most appropriate in this case.

You think so? sneered Manari. Look, if you want some peace in this village, then you had better leave the police out of the matter. A man deals with a small domestic problem his own way and they want to run him out of the town. Look, if any of you squeals, he dies and I say this as an oath over the blood of my mother.

Manari spat on the dusty floor and went out. The old men stood looking at each other. There was nothing they could do, since nobody wanted to die. In any case, the boy's father and mother had been publicly disgraced for stealing in the past. There was no point pursuing the matter further.

People whispered behind Manari' s back, but not one confronted him. Weeks later, the peace of the village was again disturbed when truckloads of soldiers trooped into the community. They were looking for members of vigilante groups, especially those who were associated with the popular political activists. Okoke put up a stiff resistance and the invading soldiers got angry. Little hamlets around Oroke were razed to the ground and thousands were rendered homeless. At dawn, the soldiers would invade the village. The old men and women who were unable to run away sat on the bare ground or on low stools with misery inscribed on their sun blackened faces. The old folk heard rumours that the youth of their community wanted to bring down the government in the city. Little children huddled between their knees. Young men who tried to flee into the surrounding bushes were shot in the back, their petrified arms stretched towards the indifferent skies. Blood on the paths, tears on the thresholds of doors and tobacco stained spittle virtually everywhere. Vultures hovered over ruins of the burnt hovels and pecked on the corpses that hadn't been disposed. Dogs competed with vultures over the corpses. Tani hid indoors almost totally paralysed by fear.

Maniyan went to the market at about noon during the siege. She had gone to buy some yams and also condiments to make a pot of soup. There were some soldiers sitting on the branches of some thickly leaved trees. Maniyan had to pass in front of the trees as she returned back home. She walked with haste even as she carried a basket on her head. There were two women a few steps ahead of her. As they got nearer the trees on which the soldiers were seated, Maniyan found herself succumbing to a mounting feeling of fear. Four soldiers armed with obsolete and ugly looking submachine guns jumped off the stems of the trees. Three of them started to laugh coarsely while their leader barked out orders at the frightened women.

Where do you think you're going, don't you know there is a curfew?

We thought we still had enough time to get to the market.... the day is still very bright?

You're talking and looking me in the eye!

Lie down, you bitches! snapped a soldier who was wearing a pair of cheap yellow rubber slippers.

We're sorry, sir.

Maniyan stood several paces behind, watching. A troop of vultures swam clumsily across the sky. They had been nearby since the last massacre.

What do you have in your bags? shouted the leader.

Things to make to make a soup.

So you still have time to eat while your village burns?

Is that right? asked the soldier wearing the pair of cheap yellow slippers.

We are starving, sir.

Starving? How won't you starve when you're a bunch of lazy idiots?

In fact, I wish you would all starve to death!

The leader poked their baskets with the tip of his submachine gun and found a few pears. He picked up one and threw the others to his men.

These bitches just enjoy themselves while the rest of the country wastes away.

Yeah boss, said a soldier who had tribal scars all over his face.

The leader poked into the basket again with his gun. A bunch of wilting spinach didn't appeal to him. He kicked one of the baskets and lumps of potash spilled onto the dust. The kneeling women trembled all the while.

Shut your eyes, bitches, yelled the soldier who was wearing the pair of yellow slippers. His fly was only half done and his blood red underwear glimmered beneath the pale sunrays. The leader fondled the breasts of the younger woman roughly and she balked.

The rest of the men broke out in laughter.

Don't you like it, bitch? he snapped, also laughing. The woman said nothing, but there was a slight frown on her face.

Answer me now, snarled the leader fondling her breast roughly again.

This time she tried to cover them with her arms.

Why are you hiding your melons away from me? Tell me, my dear.

His uneven yellow teeth glinted in the failing sunlight. The older woman began to sob quietly. Maniyan stood stock-still. There was no point retreating. They had all seen her.

Look at this one, he said jabbing the sobbing woman on the breasts with the barrel of his gun. She almost fell over and then he held her off the ground with a huge boot. The soldiers burst out laughing.

Her breasts have shrivelled up. She's useless now, he said turning to the men.

Please leave her alone, pleaded the younger woman.

I'll be alright, countered the older woman.

Get up, said the leader to the older woman.

Please…. said the younger woman

Please, said the older woman.

Shut up, you bitches. You, bawled the leader to the older woman, hold your ears and run now! Do you hear me? I said run away now as fast as a dog or else I will shoot you!

The woman looked at her basket and its scattered contents. Her gaze drifted away from them quickly and turned towards the direction of the village.

I'll see you at home, mama, said the younger woman. The older woman didn't walk away fast enough and so she was kicked on her buttocks.

Old cow, cursed the soldier with the yellow pair of slippers. The woman walked faster clutching her hurting waist.

I think I should keep this one for myself, said the leader to his men.

I can see you know what is good for you, said the soldier with the tribal marks on his face. The young woman began to get even more apprehensive.

I have a husband and two children at home, she muttered.

Shut up! Who asked you anything?

Please, sir.

Is your husband a man? If he were a man he would be here to save your lousy neck!

My children, God help me.

Forget about your shitty children! I'll fuck you in a way your husband has never done!

The soldiers laughed wildly.

Come here, bitch, a soldier shouted at Maniyan. She dropped her basket in fright and was asked to pick it up.

Just wait and let me finish with this bitch.

Oh, God.

Which God, bitch! Tell me which God? How can a devil defile the name of God?

He dragged her along the dusty path bruising her knees.

What's wrong with you, bitch? Don't you want to come home with me?

Please, I have a husband and children at home.

The vultures crawled towards the eastern part of the sky. The sun's light dimmed palpably and a cool breeze came and ate into their bodies.

Are you coming or not?

But I told you I have a husband already.

Get up! I said get up.

Please, sir.

Begin to run towards the other side.

The woman scuttled like a broken wing of an airplane.

Fire, he barked at his men.

She fell aside by a thick cluster of wild grass. Her wrap had come off undone and blood dribbled out of her mouth. A few moments later, a handful of large green flies buzzed about her.

Maniyan grew cold with fright. She felt an enormous sense of solitude. The light of the sun came on strongly again and sweat broke out on her face and upper arms. She felt her terrified eyes bulging through the chill of fear. The leader tugged at her breast and she kept still. She stood staring at her aggressor with a mixture of passivity and horror. The soldiers were waiting for another order to shoot. The vultures in the sky had drawn closer. Two soldiers took hold of her and dragged her towards the direction of the military camp. Maniyan did not offer the merest hint of resistance. The other soldiers stood watching until they disappeared behind the bushes and then they went into the village shooting happily into the pale, grey sky.

The old woman whose daughter had been killed ran to the council of elders and reported the matter. When Maniyan didn't return home, Tani and the rest of the family also presented their case before the council. The weather-worn elders shared lobes of kolanuts among themselves and muttered about maintaining patience. The meeting of elders dragged on through the evening until a battered army jeep drove to the hut where they were situated.

A major jumped off the vehicle followed by a few armed soldiers. A discomforting silence swept through the crowd that had gathered to hear what had happened.

Who is the man in charge here? said the major with both hands on his armed waist.

No one answered.

Are you all deaf? I said who is the chief around here?

There are many chiefs-- who do you want? said one of the elders.

Do you answer a question with another? Look, we are here to establish peace here, but if you want to remain recalcitrant then whatever happens to you is entirely your fault.

We want peace as well.

The government is spending a lot of money to see that there is law and order and still you insist on fomenting trouble.

We don't want any trouble. A woman was killed and another is missing, so we are discussing what is to be done.

Well, this is an illegal meeting and you all know it. I'm letting you off this time, but next time you shall all be tried accordingly and the full force of law will be applied.

We are only discussing issues that concern the safety of our people.

Well, if you have any complaints you know where the camp is. Now beat it!

The crowd began to disperse without a word. A day later, Jeremiah sat at home brooding. Maja came to see him and asserted that something needed to be done.

What can be done? You know what those military boys are like. They shoot without thinking. Or rather, they shoot first and think later.

We can't just sit on the fence in matters like this. We have to act decisively. You remember the tale about the bat?

Jeremiah nodded.

You remember how he came to be saddled with such an abominable position. If you've forgotten I shall remind you. When you look at the face of the bat it happens to look like a dog and a rat at the same time and when you take its wings into account, it looks like a bird. Yet it is neither dog nor rat.

Jeremiah knew the story very well, but there was no point interrupting Maja since he was bent on getting to the end of it.

There was a meeting that was held in heaven to which all the birds and animals on the earth were invited. The bat failed to attend and when the birds and animals returned from the meeting he started to inquire about what had taken place. First of all, he went to the dogs and was told that he wasn't a real dog because he had wings even though he had dog ears. The rats also told him he didn't belong to their group because he flew like a bird. Then he thought, ah I'll go to the birds, they would accept me. Of course they didn't because he had a little, hairy tail, a doglike face and ratlike ears. It was then that the hosts of heaven told him to wait until the world was created anew. Till then the bat has to remain hanging upside-down whenever it chooses to perch because it exists in a physical limbo. May we not be like the bat, concluded Maja

I shall go and look for Maniyan today.

That's exactly what I want to hear.

They finished the gourd of palm wine that sat on the floor and Jeremiah fetched his old rusty bicycle and rode in the direction of the military camp. As he approached it, his heartbeat grew faster, but there was nothing he could do about his apprehensions. He did not want to be called a coward by his co-villagers. He pedalled on into the softened sunlight until he was accosted by two soldiers.

Hey, where do you think you're going? queried one of them, poking him in the belly with a submachine gun. There was no one around. The other soldier frisked him thoroughly and found no weapon.

To the military camp, said Jeremiah.

Don't you know it is out of bounds? asked the soldier who had just frisked him.

We are told to report whatever complaints we have at the camp.

Who told you so?

A major.

A major? Doesn't he have a name?

I don't know his name.

Then you're a spy. Lie down you pig!

Jeremiah was violently hurled into the dust.

I'm not a spy.... I was only going to report a case of a missing person.

What's the person's name?

Maniyan.

Is she a woman?

Yes.

The two soldiers started to laugh. The astonished and scared old man didn't know why. One of the soldiers brought out a bottle of home brewed gin from one of his pockets and took a long swig, then passed it on to his mate. The other took a swig and rinsed his mouth with a supplicant expression on his face. One of the men placed the sole of a boot against Jeremiah's cheek. He didn't bother to draw away his face. A great feeling of discomfort rose from his throat.

So you want to lodge a compliant against the army because you're rich enough to own a bicycle?

No, sir, I'm a poor farmer with so many mouths to feed.

You're just an idle old man.

I only want to report the case of a missing person.

One of the soldiers got onto the bicycle and started to ride in circles until he fell off. Both men started to laugh, leaving Jeremiah in the dust still.

What do you have in your pockets?

Not much.

Not much? I thought you were rich and idle.

They both started to laugh again. The soldier who had fallen off the bicycle got on again and rode very fast in the direction of the village and then swerved around.

So you want to report the army? What nerve, you're all ingrates! The army is supposed to protect you, stupid! And you shall pay for your ingratitude and stupidity.

The cyclist drew close and braked sharply, almost falling off in the process.

This bike is still in very good shape. I think I shall keep it and go around town on it. I can ride it to the market and have fun.

Yeah, that's a good idea. Swine, would you empty your pockets?

A few coins fell out.

Is this all you've got? winced the soldier in disappointment.

Yes.

So, a poor man like you thinks he can take on the whole army? You are such a fool!

The soldier lifted him onto his feet by the scruff of his neck and kicked him by his soles towards the camp. The other soldier went on enjoying himself on the bicycle. Some vultures started to circle above the man who was being molested. The sun went down and the horizon ahead reddened as if it were a sign of bad times to come. A few other men went missing and the soldiers in the camp could not come up with any satisfactory explanation. Instead, they invaded the village randomly to ask for bribes and terrorise the people. Displaced people who had had their huts burnt hung around the huts of more fortunate people to pass cold mosquito laden nights. And then the soldiers came and warned the council of elders to stop harbouring homeless people. They were driven to the edges of the forest, where blades of grass and wild plants bristled with swollen menace.

A wild looking man emerged from one of the bushes one night and settled in with a group of displaced people. No one drove him away because he spoke the dialect with only slight variations. He had a ragged piece of loincloth around his waist and his senses were as keen as an animal's. The people who slept at the edges of the bushes were farmhands and by dusk they were too exhausted to notice any harmless stranger in their midst. Bonga, as the wild looking man was called, wouldn't eat for days when he first arrived from the bush. Anytime he was offered a piece of roast yam or something edible, he refused to accept it. It was only after he had seen his hosts eating did he begin to trust them and then did he begin to display his innate gluttony. He would want to eat everything that had been proven safe. When he caught a fish from a river nearby, he left it to dry beneath the heat of the sun until it started to emit maggots. He then ate the fish, maggots and all. Once when he had enough money, he bought a chunk of venison from the village market. He kept the meat on a stack of fresh palm fronds at the edge of the brush. Soon it became covered with ants and he ate the meat, ants and all. The ants were his since he had paid for the meat.

One morning, when the inhabitants of Oroke had woken up, some soldiers came on foot and started to harass them again. The soldiers were reeking of alcohol as they fired bullets from their ramshackle guns into the air. Vultures perched on the surrounding trees and watched. Dirty, hungry looking dogs ran helter-skelter across mazes of narrow bypaths. And goats ran into themselves bleating. Young men took to their heels and hid in bushes. The unlucky ones amongst them were shot in the back. The soldiers wanted to take away chicken, goats, yam and whatnot. No one was prepared to challenge them effectively. Old people sat watching with sad mute eyes. The laughter of the soldiers cracked through the disturbed air as they raised thick dust chasing after frightened, bleating goats. Chickens had their necks twisted and were thrown into sacks.

Tani knew she couldn't stay much longer. She wished her family affairs would be sorted out so that she could go back to the city and continue her existence. Everyone was sad, but she appeared the saddest. Only the chiefs were a bit content because they had received some monetary inducement from the military headquarters that was located in the next major town.

Tani went to see Maja two days later, after the latest military raid. It was evening and she found him sitting on the ground with a loincloth tied around his waist. People came and went before him and he continued to sit in that position, bulging. He discussed serious matters with quite a number of people. The rains, the raids, the changing times and dead people whose ghosts people fed with yarns.

I want to go back home, I'm tired of staying here, said Tani.

This is your home, you've got no other home.

The kids, they have to go to school and get what they need to become useful.

Any child who will be useful would be and there's nothing anybody can do about it

The point is that I want to go home.

You will when matters have been decided.

Look at the way the soldiers are carrying on.

It isn't their fault, since we allow them.

What do you mean?

Look, there are some so-called bloody chiefs that have actually invited the soldiers to go about burning people's houses. They pay them to do so.

Is that true?

You're damned right it is. And that old wizard Menkine who is arguably the most evil man in this village is also involved. I thought he was strong enough to carry out his vile acts alone. Now he has employed those mindless soldiers to assist him. Isn't it shameful? Everyone is just praying for his death.

It may be a good thing if he dies.

You had better hold your tongue. You can never be too sure if his spirits are hovering around here. You have got to be strong… you need a strong head to withstand his psychic assaults.

I know.

I know, but I don't want you to be exposed to any unnecessary danger.

What can be done?

The rot has got to wipe out the whole lot of us and then we can begin from the ashes of death, if that is possible.

Tani was impressed, but she thought he was being too pessimistic.

I've heard about the havoc that Menkine is wreaking, she said.

Oh, he is a thoroughgoing bastard but he's got guts. Children don't dare sit next to him in church. When they see him coming, they cling to their mothers' gowns like fleas.

Is that so?

He's that bad. The only person that is as cruel as him is that witch of a loan shark who stays in that yellow storey building on the other side of the village.

Really?

Once Menkine pretended he was dead and got his family to stage a mock burial. Everyone came to his house to see his corpse. Drummers struck their gongs in merriment and dancers trooped out to the village square. The still body of Menkine was wrapped in a white shroud. Some imprudent people thought it was a chance to abuse him and did so to his hearing. Menkine waited. When everyone present had filed past him, he stood up and pandemonium broke loose. People scampered screaming, "ghost ghost ghost !" Of course it was no ghost but Menkine himself. Those that had abused him were visited by his boys who slaughtered all their livestock.

He's such a terrible man.

He'll do himself in one of these days, Maja said, scratching where a mosquito had bitten him on his thigh.

He thinks he is very clever and he is, in fact, but he's going to get it one of these days. Remember the story of tortoise and his cleverness. There was supposed to be a meeting of all the animals on earth and in heaven. The tortoise went to the ostrich to borrow some feathers so he could fly to heaven, but he was refused. So he went to the other birds; doves, hawks, owls, falcons, eagles, pheasants, parrots and what have you and they gave him each, a feather. On the appointed day, they all flew to heaven. Before their flight to heaven, the tortoise had told them that his name in the celestial realm was "All of you." That was the name an angel is going to call him. Every bird accepted it. In heaven a feast was laid down for them. "All of you" come and eat said the angel and the tortoise alone got up and went into the immense dining hall that was large enough to accommodate creatures from all the continents of the earth. There were many dishes on the dining table. In fact, more than enough for all creatures both living and dead and he proceeded to help himself to each one of them. When he finished he joined the rest of the birds, who were starving. They complained to the angels and were told they had all been invited to eat. But of course the tortoise had already had the best part of the feast and what he could not devour, he defiled. So the birds ate whatever crumbs they could find and then took back the feathers they had lent the tortoise. They all flew back to earth and left him with the angels because he had been very greedy. He begged and begged for the birds to forgive him, but they wouldn't budge. So he went to the edge of the heavens and looked at earth, which was far down below. He shut his eyes and jumped off the edge and sailed leagues upon leagues downwards until he crashed on his back. His shell got scattered. To cut a long story short, he got a colony of ants to piece together his scattered shell in exchange for chewed upon bits of sugarcane. Those that seek to be too clever at the expense of others always end up badly.

When he looked towards the left side, Maja saw a woman of about fifty approaching him. She was a widow who worked on a farm for a living. When there were any social events, she sang and danced for a women's cultural troupe. She stopped a few paces away and frowned. She didn't say anything. Tani scanned her figure rather contemptuously and took her eyes away.

What's the matter, woman? Maja asked.

I hear you are the father of that motherfucker Manari, said the woman with a coarse voice.

A few women in the compound were busy going about their ordinary chores. One had gone to fetch a mortar and pestle. Another was opening the door of the chicken coop.

You're very wrong. He's only an in-law.

Very well, all the same, that saves me the trouble of visiting that family of his.

You had better watch what you say, Tani said hissing.

The women in the compound all looked up with keen ears.

Look, say what you have to say and if l can help you I will, but if not, too bad.

Such a sweet mouth that boy has. He came to me and said he repaired aeroplanes with broken wings in a big Israeli company in the city.

And you believed him? he asked.

How was I to know?

Well, go on.

The group I sing with had a show to welcome the Minister of Aviation and after our bit, I was hanging out with my friends and this boy comes to say he works for a big aeroplane servicing company. That he loves me and all that. I thought he was genuine.

How old are you, first of all?

Forty-nine.

How old is Manari? he asked turning to Tani.

About twenty-six.

Twenty-six, good. Now go on with your story.

He took me all over town and ended up doing what a man does to a woman only because I believed.

So what's your problem now?

He lied to me!

What's new in that? Men have always done that to get what they want from women.

Shameless woman, hissed Tani.

Yes, chorused the women in the compound.

The woman grew restless because she wasn't drawing any sympathy.

Look, if you have nothing to say then you had better leave, we're discussing something very important.

The woman looked uneasily around her and then walked away through the path she had come. The women in the compound hit their palms together laughing.

What a foolish old woman, allowing such a small boy to take advantage of her like that.

Maja didn't bother to laugh with them. He had other things in mind. As the head of the Wenku family, he had to take care of Tani's affairs. She was younger and more polished than his wives. He looked at her bleached skin and thought it was lovely. He would really like to fuck her. She seemed so determined, so confident about what she was about. His younger brother had been much luckier than him. Now that he was dead, he could step into his shoes. He would inherit his wife, his problems and joys as custom demanded. There was nothing wrong in that. He would make his wives and sons work harder so that he would have enough to live with Tani in the city. They had to understand that as the head of the family he had to take charge, he had to make Tani's problems his own because she would become his wife. It was necessary for him to live in the city with her so that they could understand each other better and for the sake of her children. He thought about all the modern appliances he could enjoy in the city, the refrigerator, the T.V., the electric oven, the tape recorder, and he could see so many cars all at the same time. The city had changed so much since he left after his retirement from the railways. And now that he had passed his prime, he was returning with a younger wife.

There was nothing in Oroke at that moment apart from imminent death. The soldiers had ruined everything. They raped the women and carried off goats and chickens. They burnt houses to the ground and there was nothing anybody could do about it. Perhaps by the time he was ready to die, peace would have returned to the village. For now, Tani was his only hope. He looked forward to playing the role of Ayimola's father. Most of his own sons were bums. He had heard of Ayimola's intelligence and ambition. It would be nice living with him. Such were the thoughts that occupied him until his eldest wife distracted him.

When are you going to get up from the ground or do you want the sand to eat away your genitals?

Are you talking to me? Maja was startled.

Yes, you've been sitting on your exposed backside all evening even in front of this pretty young lady.

Abomination! Disgrace! I can't believe this. You, my eldest wife talking to me like this in public? Okay since the sand is going to eat off my genitals then you are relieved of the burden of sleeping with me!

I didn't mean it that way, said his wife.

You have said what's on your mind and I have said mine so there is no need to complain. I'm not sleeping with you ever again, but I'm not stopping you from sleeping with any man of your choice once you have introduced him. Is that okay?

His wife was confounded. She didn't expect that he would react in such a manner. But she knew her man. Nothing would make him change his mind. She was glad she had already all the children she wanted, nine in all, and she was past childbearing age.

Maja told Tani that he was coming to the city with her as the head of the family. Tani on her own part thought she would have to show him how foolish he really was. An old man coming to embroider the last threads of his miserable life in a city whose intestines he could never understand, one whose language was bound to confuse him with its innumerable labyrinthine inflexions. Fuck the family! Fuck Oroke and its blind meaningless customs! She was going to demonstrate to him that he couldn't have been more wrong in his decision to come with her.

Part III

Ayimola went to stay with his biological mother after the death of his father, but when his new father Maja, came to live in the city he moved back into the Wenku household. They found a little bungalow in a middle class part of the city. The shantytowns weren't too many yet in their new neighbourhood. Ayimola was still hoping that he would achieve real success as an artist. He wasn't sure what direction his art would eventually take, but he kept in touch with bohemian artistic circles waiting for the spark that would develop his talents even further. And then he met Henrietta John-Davies at an art exhibition she held in a more prosperous quarter of the city. It had been organised by a few Swiss citizens who were resident in the country. Henrietta's mother was Swiss. She had studied fine art in Paris and had come back breathing the fire of life. She had craved to revolutionise the entire art scene. Henrietta took an immediate liking to Ayimola because he listened to her. He appeared so childlike, so cute with his shy smiles and awkward movements any time she was around him. She had two lovely daughters, Tandi and Sheena who had what Henrietta called mother fixation, "mum addiction". They lived in a small flat not far from where he lived. The whole place was filled with artworks: Yoruba masks, Tiv carvings, Benin bronze works as well as artefacts from the Northwest of the country. The high wood divider where the TV set was, the floor and the walls were all cluttered with masks, wood carvings, pieces of sculpture, oil paintings and watercolours. Henrietta made sure art took up everywhere. Little mice would run out of her studio and run up the divider into the masks and earthenware pots. She loved rock music, techno, kwaito, music from Cape Verde, North Africa, Mali and the Caribbean. She even hoped that her daughters would become musicians. She was also very political and never shrank from discussing any burning social issue. Sometimes she even wrote fiery articles concerning the state of the nation in the news magazines and journals. Oftentimes, she tried too hard to be everywhere and in everything. At over forty she was still a firebrand, she wanted socio-political change, real drastic reform so that the black man could be truly liberated, so that he could walk with other races on the basis of equality and self-pride.

We're fucked, she would say.

What can one do? he asked sheepishly. He was always in awe of her. He just could not understand why she had taken a fancy for him.

We just have to get our shit together. Can't you see what is happening in some Asian countries? Latin America, the whole fucking world is already in the future and Africa is nowhere yet. It's such a fucking shame.

Ayimola couldn't agree more. The horrifying spectres of hunger, disease, internecine strife, genocide and what have you. The burning shit of not being able to forge ahead, to organise and walk decently under the sun. Talking to Henrietta made him feel fucked up. He had been wasting his time with aesthetic concepts that were removed from the immediate concerns of his social context. Henrietta made him discern the profound disorientation. It was a form of disorientation that she seemed to have overcome even though there was a strongly bohemian nonconformist element in her personality. She wore weird clothes, eastern turbans and exotic jewellery. She was just up there for herself alone yet she couldn't shut her eyes to the need for change. She was ready to shed her blood for change. She made African-type prints with an assortment of indigenous fabrics. She had a truly unique imagination. Ayimola felt humbled by the strength and diversity of her talents, by the strength her character. It was that very strength that made him feel inadequate when compared to her.

You keep putting me on a pedestal, she says. He wished it wasn't true, but it was. He deified her almost beyond measure because she was beautiful, intelligent and immensely talented. He felt a certain powerlessness before her gifts; she was like an all-conquering hallucinogen, one that transformed him into a zero, a pathetic tabula rasa that absorbed her flamboyant footprints. He feared what might happen if he gave in so completely to her. It would be Henrietta's way and viewpoint all the time. He would be a mere vessel. He feared a total loss of self through an inordinate amount of identification with her. He could not be called an effective collaborator who attested to her femininity and whose approval and inputs were important because her self-worth was something that had been long established. He felt he wouldn't amount to much if he became a fixture in her life. But she craved him and he could not tell why. She kept offering him clear opportunities and signs to become part of her life. Ayimola would spend hours and entire nights chatting with her and he tried to adopt some of her political views. But there was something apocryphal about his political awakening if it may be called so. Whereas her own outrage had a long history, one that had become an integral part of her being, his came into existence through an emotional association and could be vitiated when those emotional ties were broken. As long as he remained with her, it was certain that she wouldn't allow him to relent, she would continue to nurture within him the seed and fire of social activism.

Ayimola was walking home after one of those long engaging nights with Henrietta. He felt the night's coolness as he drifted into the soothing rushes of wind. Then he saw a searchlight flagging down vehicles. It was a roadblock manned by soldiers. He felt slightly apprehensive because he was alone. He wasn't carrying any form of identification and if he was unlucky he could be shot and thrown into the weed-strewn canal just up the road. Without any ceremony he could be thrashed over the head with a gun butt and kicked into the swamp where the weeds would choke him to death and where no one might find him unless they became alerted by the stench of his corpse. Most of the night crawlers in automobiles were wealthy and with a few notes in hand and a generous nod, they were allowed to drive on. He felt cold around the armpits as he was hailed by the two soldiers, who kept swirling their torches in the whorls of darkness. A pungent tang of alcohol shot across towards him. Cheap home brewed gin. The soldiers were swaying within clouds of mosquitoes.

Where are you coming from?

Good evening, officers. I'm coming from a friend who is very ill, he lied. Henrietta only had a cold.

Don't you know there is a curfew?

She might die, so I had to see her.

Oh, it's a woman? You've been with a woman while we've been here enduring mosquito bites and protecting the country while you idle fuckers do as you please.

She's only an aunt.

Is she pretty?

You have to see her for yourself.

Go and sit down on the ground over there and get a feel of what we've been enjoying.

Ayimola looked at the patch of ground and he shuddered. It was by a concrete fence that had overgrown weeds and grass about it. Odious things might have been crawling in there. He was certain there would be huge rats scuttling beneath the undergrowths. He was also sure that there would be millipedes and all sorts of insects that bite. Another car drove up and attention was diverted from him. A man waved at them and dropped a half-drunk bottle of brandy into the palm of one of the soldiers. Ayimola wished Henrietta was around. She would have shouted her way out of trouble; she would have intimidated them by the aggressiveness of her intelligence. They would have coiled back because they wouldn't know where she was coming from, whom she knew. She could know members of the entire ministerial cabinet; she could have friends in the higher cadres of the army. She also had an impressive foreign accent, which was an added advantage. The soldiers were always warned to avoid injury to foreign nationals. Ayimola crouched in the darkness, resigned to fate. He had enough money to buy the soldiers who held him captive drinks, but that wouldn't have been enough to appease them. He wished he had real money. What a coward he was. Christ! He was so fucked up. Why couldn't he be Che Guevara in that drunken night of absurd soldiers? He longed for a romantic death in which heroic tales of martyrdom would shroud his name. He wished his memory would spin out waves of undying poetry for generations to come. But this couldn't be so. He would be shot in the head at point blank range and tossed into the canal like a dog. There was no fucking poetry in that! No novelty, only miles and miles of banditry and banality that wouldn't have the fortune of being acknowledged by even the most depraved kind of historiography. It would be such a meaningless way to die. Disembowelling oneself would be more courageous-- there was a loaded symbolism in it. But those soldiers couldn't care less, they would banalise his death and abolish its significance through the pervasiveness of a mindless routine and by violent and reckless expenditure. Their very presence had eroded the power of lyricism, of history, of rational invention and had turned life into a matter-of-fact scenario of random sparks, romanceless ordinariness.

Please allow me to go. I'm totally harmless.

How do we know that? No harmless person would be walking about at this time of the night.

Okay, I won't let it happen again.

You bloody civilians are always trying to create divisions within the army. You've been behind all the recent mutinies and coup attempts.

God forbid! I'm not involved.

You have to come with us to the barracks to prove that!

And you know what that means, you'll be locked up in the guard room in solitary confinement.

Ayimola knew he may not come out alive if he was taken into the barracks, so he intensified his begging.

Where do you come from actually? he was asked.

This country.

This country? It can't be true. We don't beg forgiveness without giving something away in return.

I haven't got much here… only enough for a drink.

The soldier turned to attend to the car they flagged down. Ayimola brought out all the money he had and held it tightly in his palm. He waited patiently for them to return to him. Fear had started to overpower him. No one could predict what they might do.

Please use this, he said when they finally came up to him again.

They ignored him and chatted with each other.

Please, please, he kept saying to them.

We don't receive bribes. You civilians spoil us. If you give me a gift, I will accept, but I want you to get it into your thick skull that we don't receive bribes.

I know you don't receive bribes. What I'm giving you is only a gift.

They took what he gave them, but when he tried to go, they prevented him. He waited for some minutes before he was finally allowed leave. He walked lazily past the canal disgusted with his cowardice. But then perhaps he hadn't exactly been a coward in dealing with those military goons, since he accepted that reason beyond them. Perhaps anyone who tried to be brave before them was only foolishly courting death. He looked down into the weed-infested canal and the stench rose up to his nose. Shitty rain water and mountains of refuse. Then he came to a herd of sheep. The smell of sheep urine shot through his nose. By dawn, they would have been removed by the shepherds who tended them. He went on until he reached the last bend of the road that led to the house in which he lived. He brought out the keys to the gate and went around the bungalow to the servants' quarters where Otabolo had his room. Otabolo had been retained by Tani even though she didn't really like him. But she needed him to do the household chores.

Ayimola knocked on Otabolo's door and received no reply. He knocked again and heard him sigh as he shifted on his bed. Otabolo then opened the door and came out naked. Ayimola teased him about his nakedness as he squinted in the darkness.

I almost got killed just now.

Just then a cracking report of machine gun fire was heard.

See what I mean. Two drunk soldiers are stationed at a roadblock at the other side of the canal.

They are not fit to live in the midst of human beings, they're just a bunch of beasts, said Otabolo.

I was with Henrietta. She wouldn't believe how close I was to death. I love that woman.

Why don't you marry her?

I've not really thought about it. And she already has two kids. Besides she's older than me, much older, he said laughing.

That shouldn't be a problem.

I was only joking. But her standards are so high.

Make her know that you love her.

She knows.

How can you prove that?

She's no fool. I go there all the time.

A white and black cat crept stealthily across the edge of the fence.

There was a pause in their conversation as they both listened to whether there would be more gun shots.

I hope those bastards haven't killed somebody, said Ayimola.

They probably shot into the air.

How are the old man and his wife?

They are both fast asleep.

Good, I'm hungry.

You'll find your dinner on the dining table.

Goodnight.

Yeah, Goodnight.

Ayimola let himself in through the back door. There were pools of water on the kitchen floor that had come from the temporarily dead refrigerator. There was no electricity. A kerosene lamp had been lit and left for him on the dining table. Its fumes irritated him and the heat was oppressive. He also couldn't stand the smell of kerosene. It reminded him of squatter camps plagued by poverty and fire disasters. He opened the dishes and found some boiled plantain and onion sauce. He took a bite and the food was cold. It felt awful, but it was better than nothing. Then he thought of Henrietta and his heart warmed up. He took his half-eaten meal and the dishes to the kitchen sink. A few cockroaches were loitering on the cupboard. They scampered into their cracks when he swept a hand over them. The lid of the bin had not been properly replaced so he used his fork to push the remnants into it. At the edges of the bin, more cockroaches hung. Slowly in the half-light, he washed the dishes with a filthy over-used sponge and greasy soapy water. And then he headed for his little room at the beginning of the corridor. He opened his door and an overwhelming mustiness greeted him. Flinging himself into his bed, he signed heavily. Too exhausted, he couldn't change his clothes immediately. Drifting off to sleep, he was brought back to consciousness by the piercing whine of mosquitoes. Sweat had broken out on his forehead, but he didn't want to open the windows, since he preferred the heat to mosquitoes. Ayimola put on a pair of shorts and a dirty T-shirt. Thoughts about Henrietta returned to him. He went over all that they had said to each other and what he would tell her when he saw her again the following day.

A bitterness in his mouth woke him up. He hadn't slept well, the insensitivity of drunk soldiers during the previous night, the harshness of the heat and the oppressiveness of the mosquitoes and the anxiety to see Henrietta had all made his sleep restless. He could hear Maja fetching water from the large plastic container in the corridor. His heart sank at the thought of having to meet the old man, he was such a pain. A few sharp knocks on his door tore his fragile island of peace to shreds.

Yes? Who is it?

Whom do you think you're talking to? Open the door right now.

Good morning, sir.

Where did you go last night?

I went to see a friend.

And you know how dangerous it is to stay out that late now?

I do, sir, but I don't go to any unsafe areas.

No area is safe in this city! The whole place is swarming with armed robbers and vicious soldiers. Crime has taken over the land. I don't know how anyone could choose to be so insensible.

I'm sorry, sir, I won't let it happen again.

As the head of the family, I expect to be obeyed. You give me problems and so does Tani. She wouldn't accept me, but she's the one who would be worse off for it.

Tani would never accept him. Ayimola heard them having an argument a few nights back. Maja had gone to her bedroom door.

Please open this door now, he had been pleading.

Go back to sleep you, shameless old man.

But I love you… please, I'm now your husband.

You are not.

Please open this door for the good of this family.

No, I won't.

Ayimola wanted to move out to the house so that he wouldn't have to listen to such things and so that no one would keep telling him how to lead his life. He hated having to live with people that didn't bother to understand him. He also wasn't impressed with the sort of lives his hosts were living. Their lives had nothing in common with his ways. He hated his father for having had him out of wedlock. He hated his mother for not being strong enough to raise him alone. Most of all, he hated himself for not having sufficient financial independence. More precisely, he hated the fact that he was compelled to live with people he did not love or respect and worse still, for whom he had nothing but scorn. He had been left alone to find his way in a hostile world. He would have to climb out of the thorn filled hole by himself, relying on his wits and good fortune. He was sickened that he had to kow-tow to Maja, the barely literate senile fool who had committed the greatest blunder in his life by taking up Tani and moving back to the city. He had irrevocably wrecked his family and now he wanted to ruin Solomon's.

Ayimola waited impatiently for nightfall so he could visit Henrietta. Nothing could ever stop him from visiting. She was his strength, his light of understanding, his reason for living. Her words were the emotional and medicinal shots that kept his fragile life afloat. Henrietta's world opened up expanses of sunlight where he could hear music tingling on the bright edges of immense possibilities. Within her light, his past did not matter. It was only the future that was of importance. She pounded the hardness of her words into his decadent indifference. He was reduced by an indifference he had nurtured without understanding the real meaning of his peculiar reality. And until he understood it, he would continue to drift in that nondescript greyness he had unconsciously made the broad feature of his drifting life. But Henrietta also made him feel so inadequate. So much brilliance contained in one person and what's more, he was always nodding in agreement to everything she said. Wasn't it a shame? And weren't her very brilliance and power instruments for domination and corruption? Could she exercise the discretion to hold herself back when she was going too far? He desperately wanted to see her all the same.

When he got there, Tandi was singing and dancing in the living room. She held on to the leg of a doll, which she used as a microphone. A huge Congo mask loomed over her. Her mother was sitting on a large fluffy couch.

I'm gonna be bigger than Madonna, Mum.

Sure you are, baby.

Ayimola sat there feeling slightly embarrassed. Or rather he was feeling sheepish as usual. As a child, he hadn't much self-confidence and now there was a little girl dancing and singing away before him like a miniature pop superstar.

Isn't she great? Henrietta asked him.

She is lovely, absolutely wonderful.

He wished he had her free and easy spirit, but he had tasted bitterness much too early in life. He had virtually no protection from the knocks and bruises that fill human existence. Tandi went on dancing away.

When he couldn't bear the embarrassment any longer he mumbled, How was your day?

Beg your pardon?

How was your day?

Oh, the usual thing. One just spends the time banging one's head against a brick wall. Same old shit!

Henrietta took a sip of herbal tea from a mug she had on a hand carved stool beside her.

Want some herbal tea?

No, thanks, but I wouldn't mind just ordinary tea.

Georgina!

Georgia emerged from the kitchen. She was Henrietta's maid and she was pretty. A girl of about seventeen years old.

Bring Ayimola some tea.

Yes, ma.

I'm trying to hold an exhibition at the Gallery of Modern Art and those arseholes that administer the place have been stalling.

I'm so sorry to hear that.

Oh, it's alright. The whole fucking system doesn't work. An artist can't even make a decent living in this society. Those conservative monkeys. Imagine just because I shave the hair on my head they think I'm irresponsible. My talents would stand out in any part of the world.

I'm sorry Henrietta… but I'm sure something can still be done.

Well, I'll keep pestering them, but if it doesn't work I'll see if the Swiss Embassy could arrange something. They like my work besides I'm half-Swiss, you know.

You are lucky.

How can you call anyone lucky in this collapsed society? The entire place has gone to the dogs.

You still manage to pay your bills from what you do. I can't.

That's because, Ayi, I have paid my dues. I'll bang my head on those fucking doors until they open up. In another society, Ayi, you would be big and all the young girls would be falling over you.

A surge of pleasure coursed through him. He was so glad she liked him. Georgina brought him a mug of hot tea. She placed it on the centre table just in front of him. The table was decorated by a bulbous vase of fresh flowers. At the corners of the room, there were potted plants. They looked quite impressive against the backdrop of white walls. A painting hung obliquely on the wall backing the television set, a present from a friend. He took a sip of his tea and it scalded his tongue.

Some people think you're a punk.

They are complete ignoramuses. When they say punk, they don't even know what it means. Punks live in Europe, in the West, but I'm totally Afrocentric without being primitive. I recognise the fact that I have to deal with an utterly modern world. I also know that certain indigenous African customs are simply barbaric and ought to be discarded. You dig?

I'm also Afrocentric.

Are you sure? You niggers are always denigrating your culture, you can't stop trying to be white and it's so shameful. When I hear a black man trying to speak like a European or an American I just think, God he's fucked. Naturally I have the foreign accent of my background, but you don't have to feel inferior when dealing with me because your experience is also very important. You dig?

What do you think about the art scene?

It's very confusing. Western collectors want us to keep churning out sentimental trash about the African past, the usual mother and child themes, market scenarios, mad colourful urban chaos and whatnot. And the terrible thing is that those Negritudist platitudes keep selling abroad for Christ's sake! You can't keep producing that kind of junk whenever. And then there are some copycats who are aping Western forms and traditions uncritically. Abstract Expressionism has become kind of old fashioned. I'm not a fashion or fad freak. I create my own style, but I also try keep in touch with what's happening on the scene.

Impressive.

Oh, Ayi, you're so impressionable. I don't think you should be in this environment. You appear to be so vulnerable. You're like a child. These brutes here would gobble you up bones and all. Do you know what comes to my mind when I think about you? I see you just gliding slowly over a bullet-strewn field. I mean you're practically running through a place where a vicious shoot out is happening and you've got no protection, darling.

He thought about it and felt quite vulnerable.
I really… like you… Henrietta.

What are you going to do about it then? She smiled.

Don't know, I almost got killed last night.

Really? What happened?

I stumbled into a couple of drunk soldiers and they were going to do something terrible to me, perhaps kill me.

Oh, I wish I had been there! I would teach them not to molest innocent people anymore. Fucking shit heads. A couple of days ago I was in a taxi on my way to catch an appointment downtown and these cops stopped me. Fresh faced boys. They wanted to conduct a search on my person so I asked them for a warrant. They couldn't provide one so I sat down in the cab waiting to see what would happen next. When they still insisted they wanted to frisk me I told them I was fucking old enough to be their mother and that I would slap them if they continued to provoke me. I made such a fuss that they started calming me down. The cab wouldn't start so they had to push it and in the end they made themselves my friends. Such arseholes. Bloody cowards.

You should think about your safety, Henrietta. Those cops are completely without sense. They would shoot at the slightest opportunity. As they say, they kill first and think later.

We have to begin a process of change. If not, there would be no salvation for this society. We have to begin the fight from somewhere and if some of us have to lose our lives in the process, then so be it, but we would have created a safer environment for our children.

What was she doing with him? He saw tears streaming down her livid cheeks and couldn't believe it, the passionate level of her involvement. She was no fraud, the system was getting to her, but she couldn't turn her eyes away from the rot. She had to confront it with all the passion she was capable of. It was incredible that anyone could insist on turning around a hopeless case. Simply incredible. Ayimola looked at the gleaming white turban she had around her bald head, he also observed the solid twinkle she had in her eyes and thought she might have been the queen in a harem full of eunuchs. She was wearing a long colourful gown made of different fabrics, *kente, adire, aso ake*, and patches of khaki. She looked so striking even with the tears flowing down her face. He was sitting beside her on the fluffy couch, basking in the pungent smell of her perfume, very feminine but also dominant, a combination that blended well with her character. He wanted to hold her, but he wasn't sure of himself. How would she react? He felt like a complete imbecile. He was dejected because he couldn't find an appropriate way to comfort her.

I know you like me, she finally said, and I like you too very much… I'm a modern woman and I'll encourage you if you feel… you know, a little hesitant.

She held his hand to feel the texture of his palms. It felt soft and she was impressed. It had a slight metrosexual feel. Quickly he withdrew his hands.

Why?

Oh, nothing.

Are you nervous?

No, on the contrary, I feel very comfortable with you.

She wanted to respond to him, but didn't and then she looked for a while at the Congolese masks on the wall. Would she ever find a man who could truly understand her? One who didn't feel unduly intimidated by her? She thought Ayimola was angelic, she had a hunch she could trust him with her children, that he would understand the nature of her work and her various battles with society. Maybe she was wrong, many men had failed her in the past but she was still willing to give him a try.

I'm leaving, he said.

Goodnight, my dear.

Tandi followed her mother to the top of the landing to see him off.

He went slowly down the stairs with a hand running down the banisters. She had a quiet eager longing in her eyes. Her body seemed momentarily numb. Tandi waved at him and he waved back. He felt quite sad with the inconclusive air that loomed over them and so did Henrietta. He looked at the frayed grey shirt he had on and he felt ashamed. When he looked at the battered pair of boots he had on, he felt even worse. She, on the other hand, had so much style; she was so developed as a personality. He cursed his poverty and his probable lack of drive for his lack of discernible style. To have her, he knew, he would have to make extraordinary sacrifices. He didn't want a short-lived affair. Nothing would be more vile and degrading. He wanted to enrich her life just as much as she was certain to enrich his.

He walked slowly towards home. A craving for a cigarette overwhelmed him. Henrietta thought smoking was a disgusting habit. What would she say if she saw him by the low life roadside stall from which he bought the cigarette? She would probably think he was cheap, that he had no self-discipline. He perceived her presence around himself. There was something tyrannical about the feeling. He had begun to judge all his actions through her lens. He seemed to weigh all his personal thoughts and acts through her powerful emotions, passions and moral judgements. It wasn't very healthy and he knew it. Such was the power she had over him. He dragged on his cigarette and blew the smoke towards the slowly blinking yellow security lights in the house on the other side of the road.

When he got home, he did not bother to disturb Otabolo and went straight to bed. Sleep didn't come immediately and images of Henrietta kept entering his field of vision. Again he didn't sleep well. He couldn't figure out how he wanted his relationship with Henrietta to turn out. Should he take the plunge and let things just ride or should he back out?

At dawn, he heard Tani digging into the earth to retrieve some of the yams she had buried in the soil because they had been prematurely harvested. She was singing religious songs in her rather strained, high-pitched voice. Lokuma was sleeping in the corridor. Maja sat on a wooden dining chair gnawing on a chewing stick. Beside him was an old rusty can that he spat into from time to time. Ayimola located all of them in his mind's eye. The sweaty smell in his room began to oppress him, so he got up to open the window. The morning air was staid, it would take some time before the freshness of nature would engulf his little dingy room. He wanted so badly to have a drink of water, but he dreaded the thought of meeting Tani or Maja, who was sure to reprimand him for coming home late the previous night. He turned on the radio to catch some early morning music, but a presenter was making some public announcements, so he turned it off. He wished a wind would gather in strength and blow through his window but no wind came. He felt really oppressed.

Sukuma! Sukuma! Go and have your bath! he heard Tani shouting.

And you, Lokoma, come and get me some groundnut oil for breakfast!

He knew Tani was about to make a breakfast of boiled yam and fried eggs. No big deal since she was no expert at frying eggs. The only consolation was that electricity had been restored. Perhaps later on in the day he could listen to some R&B tunes on the radio. He stretched out on his bed and perceived even more sharply the mustiness of his sheets. He would have to wash them soon. He hadn't washed them because the water supply had been rather inconstant. It was a task he wasn't looking forward to and he was too broke to pay a washman.

Let me see the oil you bought, he heard Tani say to Lokoma.

You're such an idiot! Can you see it is adulterated? You want to have us poisoned in this house. Couldn't common sense tell you that there are all sorts of fake stuff in the markets nowadays? Fool!

Ayimola was further dispirited by having to make do with adulterated groundnut oil. Tani would have an excuse if the eggs turned out doubly bad. In any case, Maja was too senile and imbecilic to stand up to her.

Ayimola waited until the children had gone to school and Tani was out pursuing government contracts before he went into the kitchen to have breakfast. Maja was having a midmorning nap in his bedroom. After breakfast, Ayimola went back into his bedroom to listen to some music on the radio. He prayed silently for nightfall so he could go and see Henrietta and her kids.

When he got to see her, she complained about not being able to fulfil herself.

Nothing works here. It is a place of rot, carcases and carnage. I'm entitled to a Swiss passport and if push comes to shove I'll just pack my bags and leave, damn it!

Ayimola's heart sunk. What would happen to him? How would the lopsided system be corrected if the best minds keep leaving? Who would repair the damage done by the brain drain?

Why don't you start a movement or something? He asked.

Who would join it? They'll all say that skinhead is nuts. It's such a retrogressive society and sometimes I think it's beyond redemption. Africans find it hard to prove Conrad or Haggard wrong.

He knew she would never join a movement, let alone form one because she was much too individualistic. She couldn't subject herself to the discipline that mass politically motivated processes entail.

We're not safe anymore. This morning I sent Georgina to fetch some water at the pump next door and she came back to tell me that worms were coming out of the tap. It means we could all be poisoned anytime. Imagine, worms from a tap! It's a lost battle one is fighting. Maybe I should just pack up my bags and leave.

A silence ensued.

I only hope that people like you don't crack up! You're so sensitive, she said.

I don't want you to go, Henrietta.

I've been paying my dues to see the things work out in this society, but the system only seems to favour rogues and cheats. There is no point really… I'm going to see a so-called revolutionary poet tomorrow and I'd like you to come with me. I want to prove to him that he's a bullshitter.

That's okay.

When he came the following day, he was told by Georgina that Henrietta was sleeping and didn't want to be woken up. He was devastated because it was most unlike her. He asked for a pen and note pad so he could leave her a note. He agonised over his choice of words. He wanted to hurt her in a very subtle manner. It wasn't a long note. He had to aim at a conciseness that left a lot of pointed innuendoes in between so that she gets a sense of the disappointment that wounded him. As he laboured over the note, Georgina stood close by watching him, but he was totally unconcerned with her.

Uncle, she called him as he was about to go through the door.

I'd like to have a word with you.

About what?

Can you sit down again for a few minutes?

Yes, why not.

Madam. It's about madam and you.

Ayimola was puzzled and tense at the same time.

Madam likes you very much and there are very few men she likes that way. I'm sure this isn't coming as a surprise to you. She talks about you all the time when you're not here. Are you having an affair with her?

No… erh, I guess I couldn't say so.

There was something that told him that her interest in the relationship was entirely well intentioned. Besides, she may have the clues to guide him in his future actions. Perhaps Henrietta had been talking to her, since they seemed quite close. She trusted very few people and those that were intimate with her were the only ones she confided in. Georgina was more than a mere maid, she was also a friend.

But I love her very much and she knows it… I guess you could say so.

Why don't you tell her?

Henrietta is a very complex person and I don't know if I'll be good for her… if you know what I mean.

She's actually a very simple person once you know her. Very childlike, very trusting, until you hurt her of course.

Henrietta didn't seem simple to him. He found her so interesting that he couldn't predict what she might get up to the next minute. Her dress sense, for instance, was bafflingly eclectic. Her taste in music was wide ranging and difficult to pin down and finally her impressive autodidactism in an atmosphere of entrenched philistinism made her a sort of pariah. Henrietta was clearly beyond him and his relatively humble aspirations. To be with her, he would have to redefine himself employing her criteria. She too appeared to know it. But the question was, was she willing to accept him on his own terms as he was ready to accept her completely? It was difficult to see how he would cope with the perplexing plenitude of her personality. She was as resilient as a sponge that soaked up everything. Would she be put off if she saw that he couldn't match her almost inexhaustible vibrancy, diversity and strength? He couldn't tell how she would take it when he had resigned to his natural pace of emotional and social evolution as the burning end of his life burnt itself out. He didn't want to be henpecked, to be hurled into more currents, experiences and sensations than his senses could cope with. There was a deep hunger within her, a hunger for light, a hunger for boundless adventure, a burning thirst for social change and an abiding quest to experience life lived differently. He was afraid that when he joined her along the road she was treading and he started to tire out, she would turn her restless fury upon him. He felt he wouldn't be able to find the inner strength to bear her rages and disappointment. Even if he put up a show of strength, he knew it would be exactly that, a show and nothing more. She alone would determine the flavour of the show. She would begin it and also have the honour to end it. He would be nothing but a shadow of a pretext. And then he had her kids to think about. They were so precious. He couldn't foresee how his relationship with them would end up. They had such intelligent minds and they knew that their mother loved them immensely. Perhaps they didn't want to antagonise him yet because they cared for their mother's feelings. He wasn't very good in dealing with children and had several reasons to fear that his physical and emotional clumsiness would get in the way. He had a hunch that the keen intelligence of the girls could be the nursery bed for much infantile viciousness if he made a move that did not go down well with them. If that happened, Henrietta was bound to side with the girls. She would protect them with fierce maternal fury. He remembered how they fell into her arms protectively when she was upset and crying. They tried to outdo one another showering love on her and he felt so left out, he stuck out like an intruder watching an intense family rite. He watched like a blundering fool when they kissed her tears and put their little arms around her neck. He wished he was a natural father, that he had an arresting way with children so that he could play with them without the slightest trace of self-consciousness on either side. Poor idiot that he was. But Henrietta felt strongly about him and it didn't seem to matter much. Not immediately at least. He thought about the two beautiful girls and wished there was a way he could make them accept him, make them truly love him. Nothing would have made Henrietta happier. He framed in his mind a picture of all of them holding hands, running on beach sand towards a sun bathed horizon on a fantastically gorgeous day. His heart felt heavy and there was a hint of pain in his throat. If only he could make those lovely little girls love him, if only he could fill them with laughter all the time. If he could, just like Bryan did. Bryan, a record producer, was a friend of Henrietta. He was a handsome young man with an easy manner. When he came, they jumped on him and put their arms around his neck. They smothered him with kisses, which he warmly returned.

Bryan, why don't you take us out for some ice cream, Mummy won't say anything.

I'll be so happy to do so.

He watched hopelessly as the happy banter went on. Whenever he joined in the conversation, his verbal contributions and gestures appeared laboured. Contrived. Henrietta sensed this, but she was usually understanding about his stiffness. She did her best to make him feel comfortable and he really appreciated her efforts at trying to get him integrated. He came to hold her in even higher esteem. She seemed able to read him so well. He wondered about the quality of the surprise he could come up with. He might just turn out to be a frightful bore. Someone like Henrietta needed constant high-level excitement. But how was he to continue to supply the demanding requirements of her body and spirit?

And then there was the issue of her fiery temperament. She had told him several times. "I'm a bitch sometimes, I can be really terrible". He was glad she had the courage to confess that much to him. He remembered the first time he witnessed a display of that aspect of her character. Her kids had been out playing with a friend of theirs who was slightly older. Sheena had come running to her mother to complain that she was being left out of their games and also being abused. Henrietta was furious.

Don't corrupt the minds of my girls, she yelled at their friend.

And how did you get this bruise here?

She did it… it was a mistake, she said pointing to their friend.

That's dangerous! I shan't invite you here again if you won't behave yourself. I shall report you to your mother as well.

Henrietta kept yelling. Ayimola sat huddled in a corner like a confounded boy. He didn't believe she was capable of so much fury. He watched as she paced back and forth in her little living room, walking off her anger. When she calmed down, she told him she didn't want her girls to be hurt. She had an overwhelming need to be protective of them. She had been hurt so many times and it was apparent that not all the wounds had healed. The men she had met in her life, the drinking, the drugs and beatings. It was very hard for her to begin on a clean slate. She never talked at length about it, her gaze became abstracted when she thought about her troubling past, her presence slightly removed from the moment and her voice possessed an almost painful tenderness. Ayimola knew that she had experienced a lot of heartache, full bittersweet ordeals that made life seem so short. She had undergone experiences whose lushness of colour could also be violently corrupting. He felt so honoured because she figured she could trust him. For someone like Henrietta, it was an enormous sacrifice to make. Those tears she shed when she was upset spoke volumes about old abandoned worlds, but also a hope that may be fulfilled. He sensed a keen yearning for a man. It was almost brutal. She seemed to want him to fit into her life like a missing piece of flesh, bone and spirit. It was as if she wasn't prepared to acknowledge the other ways he might have wanted to find himself within her. He felt she treated him like a cipher, that he could only realise himself completely along the lines she would draw out for him. Even though there was something childlike about her, something that opened up to wonder, certain vital rivers had frozen deep in her past and lay enveloped in the dusk. In the restlessness of her being, the past and the future collided. This curious feature of her essence bestowed her with the generosity to discern that he too had certain desires she ought not try to interfere with. As an older woman, she ought to try and nurture those desires once she ascertained they were good for him. Ayimola felt slightly hurt that she was somewhat ambivalent to that hungry part of him. She had built a frame for him and any new material he came up with was simply an aberration to her. That was almost an insult to her. Maybe he didn't have enough self-esteem and she perceived his lack of confidence, so she started to make effigies of him with which she was trying to replace his real self. It was all so confusing. Maybe he was just a canvas, malleable material on which she wanted to work according to her own artistic and psychological whims. He was glad he was able to recognise this possibility because it did a lot to boost his nebulous sense of self. The realisation that he was still capable of being critical, of producing contrary modes of reflection told him that he was also struggling to think on his own, that he was struggling to form an opinion of himself totally independent of her. It was commendable that he won back some of his independence since he held her in such self-annihilating awe. She hinted at so many things he could become through her, possibilities that were beyond even herself but it pained him that he needed her to recreate himself, to communicate with himself as it were. It also pained him that he needed her to exceed his own expectations of himself.

He wouldn't know how to pay her back, she who had given so much in the past, would give again and if he failed her, she would remain bitter till her last days. He shuddered at that possibility. Besides, he had her children to think about. If he failed her she might carry on her bitterness towards them and teach them the futility of hope. And being so precocious, they could become really cruel. He couldn't bear to imagine them turn out that way. Such beautiful little darlings. Their laughter should remain untainted during their childhood and be full of grace when the bud of youth released them into other stages of life. That way, their beauty and fullness as human beings would surpass even their mother's.

Ayimola brought up a mirror before himself and saw cracks in his image. He suspected he might have a tendency to drift from one affair to another until the frequency abolished the uniqueness of each. He feared he might become an emotionless automaton, that his life may become a concatenation of disasters. A strong woman like Henrietta could check against that eventuality. He had too much respect for her to allow himself to go to seed. He wouldn't be able to endure her fury. She had a solid focus on things. She could bear with him like an anchor against tempestuous gales and night-blue waves, against aquamarine torrential rainstorms and the frightful sight of an angry rock standing up to the fiery tantrums of a sea. And by force of habit, he too may begin to harden in the midst of flotsam. He didn't know where to turn as the still clouds of his life hung in the middle of nowhere. Each experience with Henrietta was packed with so much power that he needed time to recover and relive each alone, all by himself so they could remain fixed within him. He wasn't sure she knew the impact she made upon him every time they met. She was so intense. He needed to draw back and go over the words she uttered over and over again. He loved it when he could savour the rich emotions she provoked when she sat in lotus position on her exquisite rug telling him about life, about the necessity to refuse to be complacent in facing the struggle for the future.

In that mood, she would become so serious and it would seem to him that he was merely a victim of vague inexplicable dreams. Her words rang in the ears of his soul like a loud gong, woke him up from his passive slumber. However, he always perceived the unremitting intensity of the fight that lay before him and he felt intimidated by the prospect of waging such a demanding struggle with her alone. A fire burned within her that was impatient towards the inevitability of compromise and doublespeak. Obviously this made her somewhat helpless, vulnerable since the hardness that she cherished so much drove away so many people from seeing and fighting with her. When he too became seduced by the hardness, he found the exhortatory words of his soul stumbling and evaporating in the profound oblivion of migratory winds. It is almost impossible for a single individual to withstand such impersonal assaults. She, too, must have sensed this but it did not stop the burning going on within her. It couldn't. First, she would have to break asunder.

Ayimola hoped he too would remain keen, and interested when he reached her age instead of having to endure an indeterminateness and flaccidity that would not speak well of one who witnessed the power of fire. He decided not to see her for a while and he began to suffer from insomnia. To reduce the strength of her aroma, taste and influence in his life, he began to pay more attention to his family affairs. But it wasn't easy for him to reduce the impact of knowing her. He thought about her all the time. He missed her terribly. Words she had said to him lingered within the entire space of his being. He regretted that he couldn't fathom what her sexuality would be like. She hardly exposed any part of her body since she loved to wear baggy oriental type pants. He wondered whether she would be wild and passionate in bed or whether she would be uptight as a result of certain personal tragedies that still tormented her. Once he had seen a generous display of her leg when she sat on a cushion in her living room. Her kids had been away on a short vacation and she was alone in the flat. The electric bulb in the room gave off a faint, seductive yellowish hue that fell directly on her exposed leg. The exposed leg looked so sexual and she knew. That clean fair-complexioned leg wrapped in the telltale silence of amber. He looked at her neck and the exposed skin just below it. Her eyes became moist and touchingly desirous. He kept looking at the leg until she covered it up with her wrap. When they had nothing more to say to each other, he stood up to go. He was hoping she'd ask him to stay, but she didn't. He was slightly disappointed. Neither did she ask him to come back the following day. But he would always remember the romantic softness of the night, in the way her being sort of folded in like a little girl's and the almost painful caress of her voice. He wanted to undo the hold she had on him so that he could go on to other things.

At home, Maja and Tani weren't finding it easy to live with one another. Maja complained that Tani was failing in her duties as a wife.

Breakfast is always late. I don't know why you can't be organised.

Listen to this old man! How much do you give me to demand the right to expect so much?

A wife is a wife!

Ayimola lay on his bed thinking about Henrietta. Had she woken up yet? She was normally a late riser.

Alright then, I don't blame you, stupid old man!

Ayimola, come and get this old man off my case.

Ayimola didn't like interfering in their quarrels. He didn't feel effective doing it. Tani would sputter out so much sense and nonsense trying to see that she presented enough evidence to absolve herself of guilt. She would try to show that she had been very tolerant, more or less angelic in her conduct so far. Maja couldn't keep up with her sputtering, very few people could. A slight enigmatic smile usually played on his lips when she rambled on. He was undoubtedly overwhelmed by her rage. Soon afterwards, they settled their disagreement and for a few days or so, Tani made visible efforts to fulfil her duties as a housewife. But her mind wasn't there. She was building a house somewhere in the outskirts of the city and that was the most important thing to her. She didn't feel her future was secure in the hands of any man. Maja was not aware of the building project. He was only bothered about whether or not she cooked his meals on time.

A few days later, Ayimola lay on his bed thinking about what Henrietta may be doing when he heard some loud violent knocking on the door. Tani was away at the building site. The kids were outside playing and Maja was in his bedroom. Ayimola opened the door and two sweating women fled past him.

What's the matter?

It's Wandu! She's been locked up by the police, said a fair-complexioned woman who also on the plump side.

How come?

A woman who did not like the sight of her face got her into this mess, said the other woman.

And her sister isn't in, said Ayimola.

How about her husband? Where is he? asked the plump woman.

He's in.

Get him for us.

Indeed he hadn't heard from Wandu since the quarrel she had had with Tani. But a few mutual acquaintances had told him that she ran a thriving hairdressing salon at a seedy side of town. When he entered Maja's room, he was having a nap. He woke up the sleeping man by shaking his arm gently. The strong afternoon sun made him sweat and there was a smell of dirt and perspiration in the room.

Two women are here to see Tani, but since she's not here, they'd like to see you.

Couldn't you see that I was sleeping? I don't like to be disturbed when I'm asleep.

I'm sorry, sir, but it is very urgent. Your wife's sister has been locked up in a police cell.

Which one?

Wandu.

Oh, that troublesome one. What can I do about it then?

Why don't you see the women first?

Maja was somewhat glad that he would have something to draw him closer to Tani. He would give her his moral support. She needed it and then perhaps would come to have a higher regard for him.

What's the matter? He said, as he stepped into the cramped living room.

Good afternoon, sir, it's Wandu, your wife's sister. She's being put in a police cell.

A police cell? That's incredible.

A wicked woman who has a shop next to her did it. They are competitors and Wandu was gaining the upper hand until the other woman thought it best to put her away by buying off the police.

How unfortunate. We'll go and see her tomorrow morning.

We have to get going right away because we have to take her dinner to her. You know that the lousy meals they serve there aren't even fit for cockroaches.

Yes, I know, and thanks for everything. See you tomorrow.

Tani returned with an upset stomach. She went straight in and changed into a pair of cotton shorts and T-shirt. While Ayimola narrated what had happened, she turned, twisted and moaned on her bed.

It's so hot, she kept saying.

When Ayimola finished, she said she was going to teach Wandu's adversary that she too could pull off a few extralegal tricks.

I'll show them, she said, they'll know that we don't come from a wretched family. I'll pay whatever I have to, to see that she gets out of jail.

The following morning, Tani and Ayimola paid Wandu a visit, but they weren't allowed to see her. The security arrangements were a bit tighter than usual. The police yard was extremely filthy, like all of them were. Children of cops sold sweets, cigarettes, locally brewed gin, groundnuts and lukewarm bottles of soft drinks. They looked filthy and their clothes were ragged and torn. In front of the police residential building that stood beside the administrative block, a long open sewer continued to collect garbage: sweet wrappers, cigarette butts, empty bottles, rain water, dust and spittle.

Just as Tani and Ayimola got there, about fifteen men were brought in a large black truck. They were bound in chains at their ankles and linked to one another. They were a real chain gang. They held up their hands above their heads. A policeman who manned the gate told Tani that they were robbery suspects and would probably be executed without trial. Tani was stunningly dressed. She knew she had to impress the police to secure Wandu's release. In the yard, there were several carcasses of vehicles that had begun to get rusty. They were vehicles that had been seized from suspected robbers and smugglers. Some of them had been taken from motorists without valid vehicle particulars. If cases of vehicular theft are not resolved, the automobiles are sold off cheaply at auctions.

Mucky waters ran in the gutters that ran along the sides of the building. A loud piercing scream tore out of one of the buildings, a wail that was conversing with death. Tani asked the sentry about what was happening.

They're torturing somebody, he said, They are probably shoving the spoke of a bicycle wheel into his pee-hole.

How disgusting.

The life-numbing scream tore out of the building again and Ayimola felt like leaving. He looked at the faces of the policemen and they looked drained of feeling. He saw only greed, a greed that wiped out all traces of compassion. He was put off by the powerful stench that rose out of the gutters. The smell of urine hung about the entire yard. He just wanted to leave. Loitering around the compound were barristers looking for cheap criminal cases. They looked hungry in their frayed mournful dark legal suits. Quite a number of them weren't properly dressed. All sorts of people milled around hoping to lodge a complaint or to see one of the inmates of the cells. They offered the policemen bribes to sort out their affairs. Tani didn't know this, so they went back home.

The following morning, they came back again. This time, Tani was even more stunningly attired. She had on a bright red miniskirt and a befittingly short jacket to match. She was more determined to see her sister. Together with Ayimola, she went to one of the buildings at the back of the cells to see the inspector-in-charge. The otherwise bare room had a few benches and tables that the policemen themselves rarely used. The floor was covered with grime and dust. By the doors, children of the policemen who lived in the barracks were hawking trays of groundnut, sweets and cigarettes. Their faces were covered with grime and sweat. Tani sent word to the inspector that she would like to see him. She sweated as she waited for her turn. The ceiling fan that hung above wasn't working. It had become black with dust. She shifted and hissed from time to time. Many minutes later, a pot-bellied policeman in mufti came and said the inspector was ready to see her. She stood up, picked up her bright red handbag and walked daintily behind him in her flat, red shoes.

Ayimola trailed behind them. They reached another ugly looking building that was just in front of the gate. A few policewomen were chatting and milling around. The counter, which stood in front of the cells around the corridor, had become disfigured with age, neglect and misuse. They went up a staircase that had a rusty banister to the inspector's office. At the top of the stairs it was possible to see the male inmates of a large over congested cell. The cells had iron bars over them and looked like a human cage, a monkey cage, more appropriately. The helpless inmates looked up through the bars like animals, dehumanised by their brutal lack of freedom and space. One could see chamber pots placed between the inmates and the stench of urine was doubly strong here. Some of the inmates lay on the floor while the others sat looking at the faces of those who came up the stairs for signs of scorn and disgust. If they felt betrayed, they hurled invectives.

Tani walked quickly down the corridor at the top of the stairs. She entered the inspector's little office and shut the door. Ayimola stood outside, waiting. A few lawyers were milling around. Inside the office, a faulty air conditioner was grunting.

Yes, can I help you? asked the inspector.

He had a permanent scrawl over his face. He had on a loosely done tie and white shirt and was impressed by what he saw.

My sister is locked up in here.

What's her name?

Wandu.

He stood up and opened the door and yelled out a name into the corridor, bring the Wandu file if you can find it.

He meandered behind the desk and picked up a bottle of whiskey beneath it. He took a big swig, screwed up the cap and tossed it underneath the desk again. He gave Tani a sudden insincere smile showing his tobacco-stained teeth. Then he was seized by a violent cough.

Take it easy, would you like some water?

No, no, no, he said, still coughing. He reached for the whiskey bottle again and took an even hungrier swig. He winced as the liquor coursed through and burned his lungs. A large hairy hand was brought up to soothe his chest just before a few knocks were heard on the door.

Come in, he said struggling.

I found it, said a corporal in mufti.

The Wandu file?

Yes, sir.

Good, give it to me, he snapped.

The man handed him the file and backed out of the room. The inspector thumbed through it anxiously while Tani took a closer look at the room. Several empty bottles of liquor littered the corners. A red well worn carpet that hadn't been cleaned since heaven-knows-when. Dirty untidy files on the desk in total disarray. Cobwebs hanging from the ceiling and faded blue walls. Grimy window panes and torn askew curtains.

Ha, it would cost you 50,000, he said finally.

What? That's too much. I don't have that much.

Such a pretty woman like you? I don't believe it.

But it's true.

Then she would have to remain here. We'll take good care of her.

You must be joking.

Try me.

Please, sir, help us.

Look, I have other things to do. Don't waste my time.

I beg you, sir.

Can I take you out then?

But I am married and my husband is standing right out there.

It doesn't matter. We can do it on the sly.

He'll know. He's very jealous.

Then I can't help you.

Please, sir.

30,000. Bring it tomorrow morning, he said, opening the door for her.

Ayimola was standing with his hands in his pocket. He looked very boyish. The inspector eyed him with unhidden scorn.

This is my husband, said Tani.

The inspector took his eyes off him. There was a little veranda at the end of the corridor where a blaze of powerful sunlight streaked inside. But the other side of the corridor was dark. A stench of decay made it seem lifeless and particularly uninviting.

Thank you very much, sir, for your help, said Tani.

Oh, don't bother. Just bring the stuff tomorrow and then we'll see what we can do.

They went towards the top of the stairs where they could look down into the human cage. A number of fixed faces were looking up at them. They seemed violated by craving, loss and ineffable pain. A pungent smell of urine rode up from the pit of the cell. A scream unravelled itself from another cell somewhere. Ayimola looked down and saw the forlorn figures, sitting, lying down and others holding tightly onto the bars. Some were cursing while others remained silent. A bright orange plastic bucket caught his eye. And then a battered, shitty bedpan. Out in the sunlight, loose films of dust hung in the air. By the gate that was open, a policeman dragged on a cigarette while scratching his groin.

We're going to get her out tomorrow.

Ayimola said nothing.

Imagine that swine wanted to take me out! What does he take me for? A cheap roadside whore?

Bastards, he cursed.

Again they presented themselves in the filthy yard. A long queue of people was waiting to be admitted. The two women who had informed them about Wandu's plight were standing outside the building in the glare of sunlight holding a bowl of food wrapped in cellophane.

They won't let us in on time. If you know somebody, it would help, said the fair complexioned one.

Tani craned her neck to see if the sentry that admitted them the previous day was around. He wasn't there. Then she went around the queue to the barbed wire fence. It had large holes, through which one could pass, but she couldn't risk it. A scream rose out of one of the buildings behind. She looked desperately for a familiar face. Then he saw one of the men who had attended to her before, and hailed him. He approached her listlessly, reluctantly, with a puzzled expression on his face. Tani opened up her hand bag and picked a crisp new note. The flap of the bag hid her hand. He came and held on to the fence. Tani put the note in his hand and began to speak quickly.

Don't you remember me? she asked.

Yes, I do, madam. What can I do for you?

Please, I'd like to get in now so that I can begin the process to get out my sister.

He seemed to think for a few seconds and then he nodded towards the gate. Tani went around hurriedly and Ayimola and the two women followed her. The policeman whispered something into the ear of the sentry at the gate, then beckoned Tani to come towards him. The people on the queue eyed her and her little crowd with outrage. Tani walked past them with her nose stuck in the air. Ayimola looked indifferent beside the two eager women who strode alongside him. They went to the counter where a few policewomen stood in the outer building.

A few people were offering them bribes. Policemen in mufti went up and down the stairs. Tani gave the policewomen some money so that the two women could give Wandu her breakfast, and then she went up to see the inspector. Ayimola stood a little away from the counter, watching. Then Wandu appeared, her hair dishevelled, the straps of her bra showing through the disarray of her blouse, her nails black and broken. A painfully deviant smile played on her face. She walked as if she had chains on her feet. She hadn't had a change of clothes since she had been locked up. Ayimola came over to the counter and held her around the shoulders and she nodded and smiled at him. One of the women handed her the bowl, which she received then retreated into the labyrinth of cells. Ayimola backed away when he saw a young lawyer he knew. The solicitor was a tall gaunt guy with a weather beaten face and deep-set eyes. He liked to pass himself off as a civil rights activist. Perhaps he was, Ayimola wasn't sure.

I'd like you to help me, he said after they had greeted each other. There's somebody I know locked up in here and I'd like you to act as our lawyer.

That's no problem. I know what it's like here. We'll see what we can do, he said, patting Ayimola on the shoulder.

They went together upstairs and stood outside the inspector's office, where they chatted. From time to time, the lawyer greeted the policemen he knew. After a while, Tani came out, escorted by the inspector, who bade her farewell and then went back inside his dingy office. Ayimola introduced the lawyer to her and she led them to another office downstairs. There, they saw the woman who had arranged to have Wandu locked up. She was reticent and possessed a mean look even with her pair of spectacles. They didn't speak to one another as they faced a dull looking policewoman who sat writing behind a small desk. Then the lawyer wrote something and handed it over to her. Wandu's adversary stood close by, tight-lipped.

Tani led her little train to an unkempt waiting room in one of the buildings behind. There, they found a policeman sitting on a bench. He seemed friendly and Tani started a conversation with him.

Why is this compound so filthy? she asked him.

It's the government's fault. It doesn't care about us.

But all police compounds are filthy, just as they all have filthy minds.

That's not true, madam. We have to do what we can to survive. We don't exist as far as the government is concerned... It is a vicious cycle.

And the inmates here... life must be more than hell for them.

It's not that bad at all. They conduct their little affairs amongst themselves.

Really?

Yes of course. If you come here at night, you'll find inmates having sex around the grounds, and in those ruined vehicles.

Men and women?

Yes, men and women, he paused for a while regarding his surprised interlocutor, it's not that bad I tell you. Once you have enough money, you can get almost anything you want. Dope, sex, you name it. Some of the policewomen even have affairs with the inmates. The longer you spend here, if you're smart, the easier life gets. The big guys amongst the inmates collect protection money and some of them see no reason to get out.

Tani felt numb. She wanted her sister out. After a couple of hours, Wandu shuffled in accompanied by two policemen. She was carrying a carrier bag that contained some of her personal effects. There were no shoes on her feet, and in the bright sunlight, she looked even dirtier. Ayimola stood up to receive her. One of the policemen who had come in with her went around and opened a drawer.

This girl is very rude, he said to Tani.

I'm not rude at all. I'm only demanding my rights, said Wandu.

You see, she wouldn't even allow me to talk.

Shut up, Tani said to her.

They all remained silent, while the policeman behind the desk wrote on a sheet of ruled paper. And then the two women who had brought Wandu's breakfast came inside. They both hugged her and told her how happy they were to see her out. The policemen led them all to the outer office located in front of the building. The woman who had gotten Wandu into trouble was waiting there. Wandu eyed her disdainfully, but was ignored. The woman's bespectacled stone-like face kept looking at the sheaf of papers on the desk in front of her. They didn't say a word to each other. Tani walked around her contemptuously; she had a mind to hiss but she checked herself. They waited while the policewoman behind the desk wrote. Several minutes went by before they were all discharged.

The case had been killed.

Wandu was taken to a waiting taxicab while Tani remained behind to tip some of the policemen and women. She had to do so since it was the custom. They smiled emptily and waved at her as she made a slow exit out of the yard. Finally she tipped the policeman at the gate and felt the full force of the sun's glare. Screams ripped apart the unreal momentary peace of the yard, followed by a sputtering report of machine gun fire. Tani entered quickly into the waiting cab and ordered the driver to move.

The cab drove through heavy traffic into the neighbourhood where Wandu lived and stopped in front of a block of flats where the two women who were her friends stayed. They made their way up a narrow misshapen staircase that was quite dark. The door was open and they walked into an untidy living room. Several people who were seated there rose to greet Wandu. Tani smiled with pride all throughout.

God, how was it?

Terrible. I don't even want my worst enemy to go through what I've had to endure, said Wandu.

Let her rest, a woman said.

I'm not tired at all. I'm only glad to have gotten out of that shithole.

It must have been terrible.

You can say that again.

So what happened then? another woman asked.

I went through hell, she slumped to the floor, the subject of all eyes. Everybody bent forwards to hear properly.

Don't you want some water? asked a voice.

No, thank you. I went through hell! When I first got there I walked into a barrage of slaps, I didn't expect it at all. It's a form of welcome.

The police did that?

No, the detainees.

Well, go on.

They stripped me naked and hurled me before the "president" of the cell. She had this massive joint burning on her lips. A great fat woman. More slaps rained upon me for not greeting her properly. I was held down by about ten women to be initiated. One of them thrust a candle up my cunt, a real vicious lot they are, you know.

She paused collapsing in laughter.

You witch, Tani smiled.

I haven't finished. They lit the candle and dropped the dripping wax on my pubic hair!

How terrible.

I was made the slave of the cell. I couldn't sleep because there was no space. The old inmates had all the privileges.

Those bloody cunts, said a man.

It's not their fault... it's what the system does to them. Actually some of them are very good when you get to know them.

Look, you will come home with me when I'm ready to leave. You've lost so much weight already.

That's true, said one of the women.

Wandu continued to narrate the details of her detention until Tani stood up to go. Ayimola, who had been idly observing, also stood up. A few women rushed into a bedroom to get some of Wandu's things. A taxi was hailed and Tani, Wandu and Ayimola sat in silence as they were driven towards home. Tani felt happy that Wandu now had reason to be indebted to her. She had assisted her in a time of great need and had reasserted her authority over her. Wandu, on her own part, felt wanted. Ayimola held on to Wandu's hand as she experienced a warm flush of appreciation.

Wandu was put in the children's bedroom, after which she had a shower. Maja came out to greet her and retired again to his bedroom. Things went easily for several days. As time went by, Ayimola sensed that Wandu liked him. She would ask him to accompany her when she strolled around the neighbourhood in the evenings or when she had to go around the corner to pick up some minor household goods. She wanted to be with him always.

Tani wasn't around most of the time to watch them because she was too busy trying to complete the building she was erecting. Nothing mattered to her except to see that her building was completed. One day, she came back late as usual to meet Maja fuming.

Are you really a housewife? he asked.

Look, if you are not satisfied, you can pack your bags and go back to the village. You've become a big burden for me.

Tani, is it me you are talking to?

Who else could it be?

I should not have agreed to have you. People warned me. You abandoned my brother and led him to an early grave. In fact, some people say that you killed him. I have ruined my family because of you.

That's your bloody business! I never said I wanted you.

Have you no pity? No compassion?

Go back home!

I can see that you are a witch. You killed Solomon and now you want to kill me too.

Tani was too exhausted to have a good fight, so she went into her bedroom and locked the door. Maja continued to complain bitterly behind her door.

Better talk to your sister. That's no way to behave, he said to Wandu.

Don't be angry with her, sir. She will change.

I hope so for her own good.

Ayimola was away. When he returned, he found Wandu waiting for him in the living room.

Where have you been? she asked merrily.

Oh, seeing some friends.

Why didn't you take me with you?

I'm sorry. I thought they might not be your type of crowd.

I don't really mind. I'll get along.

Ayimola knew it wasn't true. His crowd was too educated for her and he was afraid he would be embarrassed by her coarse conduct.

Wandu was sitting on an armchair. Her body was covered with a wrap and she placed her legs on the cushion. Ayimola sat in front of her looking at her exposed panties. They looked brownish.

He thought she was sitting that way in order to turn him on.

Gradually a bulge started to emerge in his trousers.

The man and the lady of the house had a tiff this night.

What about?

Oh, it's a long story. They'll settle.

I hope so.

Ayimola was distracted by the opening between her legs and nothing she said really interested him. He went to bed when she got up and yawned as if in great discomfort. The following night, Wandu sat in front of him chatting away with her exposed panties. He found it most unbearable. The night after, the same thing happened. He sat sheepishly in front of her spread legs while she talked on as if nothing was happening. After provoking his trouser bulges, she got up to go to her bedroom.

I've got to go and change my undies.

Great, he thought.

He talked to a few friends about Wandu's behaviour.

Pour sand into her crotch if she does it again, said one of them.

He found it difficult to sleep with the great bulge in his trousers.

Sometimes Maja was kind enough to tell Lokuma and Sukuma some bedtime stories, and Ayimola sat by one night.

It isn't good to try to be too clever all the time, said the old man, I'll tell you about tortoise and one of his bad ways and how he ended up.

The children sat at his feet looking up into his face with expectant eyes.

The tortoise and the sheep were friends. This was a very long time ago. Each time they went out together, the sheep came back home to complain that he hadn't had enough to eat, but his family wouldn't believe him. Of course this was true because the tortoise always outwitted him during dinnertime. This went on for a while. The tortoise thought he ought to absolve himself, so he volunteered to take one of the sheep's offspring out to a feast that was to be hosted by the tiger. The sheep agreed, so on the appointed day, the tortoise and the lamb went to the tiger's abode. When it was time to eat, the tortoise got out and went to an immense dining table, but asked the lamb to stay behind. The tortoise told the tiger's cubs that they should feed the lamb with dregs of palm oil because that was what it liked. And true enough, the cubs went to the backyard to the lamb where they held open its mouth and forcefully poured the detritus of palm oil into its mouth. They poured it into the lamb until it became really swollen. Then they inserted a palm kernel into its anus so that it wouldn't be able to excrete as the tortoise had instructed them. When it was time to go home, the tortoise went to the backyard to fetch the bloated lamb. At home, it told its parents that it was more than full and they also believed that it had been well fed. As the night wore on, the lamb requested to use the toilet but it couldn't because a kernel had been stuck into its bum-hole. So father sheep removed the kernel and a violent gush of palm-oil detritus rushed out of the lamb's anus. It was then that father sheep knew what the tortoise had done and resolved to break up their friendship! So, children, you see where being too clever by half leads you.

They wanted him to tell them another story, but he wasn't in the mood. His relationship with Tani kept bothering him. The old man stood up and retired to his bedroom, followed by the children. Ayimola remained behind, waiting. He had been unsettled by lust. He had had enough of Wandu's cock teasing. If she came around tonight and displayed her panties before him, he would get up with a straight face and rip them off and then he would make love to her wildly against the chair. He would remember how his father had been abandoned by Tani and let his lust for revenge take him over. He would try and locate where her beginnings as a woman started and inscribe himself there so that she wouldn't forget his name. He would curse her if she violated his rite of lust with the human trappings of her voice. And then she would fall in love with him and he would hold himself back; he would let himself be taken over by indifference and neatly arranged passions, all his actions going over her head as if she wasn't there. She would come up to him desperately trying to persuade him to find a little space within him for her and he would look over her head, over her half-naked trembling body. He would watch as the yearning of her spirits subjugated her bodily desires. Her hands would be together pleading for him. He wouldn't be openly cruel to her, he would only refuse her that little space in his heart that she demanded while she suffered the wracking agony of longing, a yearning that was both profound and undiluted. Her heart would leap out towards Tani, who would then turn a spiritual fury on him. But he would rise above its violence, savouring the surprising calmness of his heart.

Wandu returned; she drew him out of himself. She wanted to chat as usual with him before turning in for the night. She went into the kitchen and returned with a saucer of fried bean cakes. Ayimola didn't want any, so she had to eat alone. He watched her, a bit disappointed that she sat properly this time. There was nothing for him to see. But a bulge throbbed in his trousers, a bulge she didn't fail to notice. She seemed indifferent to it and kept on chatting. Then he rose up after she threw another bean cake into her mouth. Without warning, he placed his mouth against hers and tried to suck out the mush but he could only get a little. Then he placed an eager palm over her large breasts and she quickly stopped it with her hand. Confused, he begged her not to scream, not to attract any attention, he would be good to her, gentle. His body bent backwards with the sharpness of rejection, he hoped his pathetic posture would make her change her mind and induce her to inscribe herself upon him instead.

His defeat hung in the mid-air like a faint smear of odourised breath, like an astonished mouth receding into oblivion. He saw the briskness of her movements, the lightness of them hovering artfully around with the mastery of victory and freedom. A victory that carried along with it a certain light musical joy, one that was brutally indifferent to the prerequisites of his spirit and the denseness of his mood. Quickly she left the living room and disappeared into her bedroom. He sat behind, numbed by the rejection, by the truly solemn heaviness of his soul, which brought on the pathos that isolated his being, a near constant heaviness that made him supremely ludicrous. How was he to confront her tomorrow morning? He felt that he had violated himself before her. The best thing was to seek her forgiveness and understanding. He hoped she would understand. When they met in the corridor, he couldn't open his mouth properly to say good morning. The vitality of his face was drained by the sluggishness of his soul. Wandu looked at him, through the deformity of his being and injected her lightness into him.

Is it because of the little incident of yesterday that you wouldn't even greet me? Forget about it and stop being childish, she said, breezing past him.

Again, the heaviness of his soul pained and embarrassed him. He couldn't find the courage to mumble anything. All through that day, he behaved like a leaf trembling in a storm. He felt ashamed of himself.

At dusk, he asked her to come with him on a walk within the neighbourhood. She walked in front, dictating the pace. He drew up to her, looked at her face and saw the beginnings of a double chin. The sharpness of his rejection waned. He felt a bit vindicated.

I'm so sorry for what happened last night. You must agree with me that it is only natural if I'm passionately attracted to you... I didn't mean to offend you.

A frown grew out of her face. His apology had been unnecessary, gratuitous. She didn't say anything, but only shrugged her shoulders, a gesture that decisively asserted the deftness of her free-and-easy spirit. Tani suspected something must be going on between them and set out to work against it.

She told Wandu, better find a man soon or you'll just end up a frustrated old maid.

Wandu was afraid; she needed to find a husband like other girls, so she started to look out more diligently for one. Men who had stable careers and good prospects were her aim. Some drove in big flashy cars to come and see her. Ayimola watched from the sidelines. He was no longer interested in her.

Weeks later, a young man called Sejeru became her most frequent visitor. Tani wasn't impressed with him because he had no car or attractive career. He was learning printing. He didn't make much of an impression on Ayimola either. The first day Ayimola saw him, Sejeru was lying on the couch in the living room, trying to make himself comfortable. Ayimola wished Tani would walk in and see him in his despicable posture. He looked so unkempt and somewhat pathetic. Sejeru was glad he had finally found a girl from a good home. Tani agreed to foot the bill for the marriage all the same. She wanted to get Wandu off her back so she could get on with her own life.

The marriage was a modest one. It took place one Saturday in a Baptist church several miles away. Many guests from Oroke came. They were Tani's relatives and were put up in her cramped living room. Tani bought a ram and paid a couple of butchers to have it slaughtered. She also hired a few professional cooks to handle the food. Nonetheless, the organisation for the wedding was quite poor.

Even with all the guests who had come from Oroke, the church was scanty. After the ceremony, they drove home in a convoy of rundown cars for the reception. The cake arrived late after all the guests had been seated. It looked as if it had been hurriedly done, incomplete. The groom was sweating profusely and Wandu looked harassed, slightly embarrassed. She kept looking at Ayimola as if for support. His face looked worn out, uncommitted. Tani was trying hard to put up a show of joy. She had done it. Maja was inconsequential. Tani looked overdressed as she tried to be everywhere all at the same time. The master of ceremony kept making a fool of himself. No one was interested in what he was saying. They were impatiently shuffling their feet as they sat, stood and sat, waiting for the food. There was also no toast to the newly wedded couple. When the trays were brought in from the kitchen, bombed-out with broken bottles, glasses, bones, tissue paper, plastic plates, paper cups and cans of edible oil, the crowd broke with an uncoordinated chorus. More bottles were knocked over and glasses broken. The greedy ones struggled for more plates of food, which they hid underneath the hired plastic chairs. The bottles of soft drinks weren't enough to go around, so some had to make do with lukewarm bottled water. All over the floor, grains of greasy jollof rice glistened. Sukuma was primarily concerned with drinking as many cans of coke as possible. The bulge of his stomach had thrusted out his soiled white shirt and his black bow tie had come undone. He kept looking for unfinished cokes amongst the debris of plates and bottles.

There was no night party and the guests chatted late into the night about Oroke and the strange city in which they had found themselves. They could hardly sleep. Clouds of mosquitoes made sleep impossible. The couple was later driven to the groom's room in a slum quite far away.

Ayimola felt imprisoned. The lack of privacy that he had to endure totally unsettled him. He took a couple of sleeping tablets, but the bitterness of sleeplessness quavered in his blood. He got up to look at his face in the mirror and he looked aged and all worn out. Besides, he had a splitting headache. He got up at dawn to go to a friend's place for some more rest. When he got there, he knocked on the door and a drunken young man opened it. Ayimola peered over his shoulder and saw a cluster of sleeping bodies lying on the floor. There was no room for him, so he began the long walk back home with a heavy body. When he reached his home, he went straight into the kitchen to see if he could find anything to eat. He found some salad in a large orange plastic bowl. Hungrily, he scooped up a plateful for himself and started to munch. A few of the ladies had woken up and they greeted him. He grunted and continued to munch. He looked at the large bin that stood beside the dead fridge. Swamps of flies were hovering above the murky refuse, the rotting leaves, bones, chicken feathers, soggy rice, salad cream and whatnot. Disgusted, he walked into his bedroom and into more sleeping forms. He wished the disorder would be cleared up and for everyone to return to their homes. A day later, he had his wish. And then a few more days later, he came down with a bad stomach upset, diarrhoea more like it. He kept visiting the toilet. He remembered the salad he had eaten and his stomach churned. After several days he got better again and swore not to eat any more salad unless he made it himself.

Wandu and her husband came to express their gratitude to Tani for all she had done for them during the wedding. Tani enjoyed playing the role of big sister. She strove to complete the building she was erecting. Now she only needed to paint and furnish it. That would be possible when she had been paid for the government contract she had just finished executing. A man five years younger than her started to visit her frequently. Lokons had been very visible during Wandu's wedding and Tani had grown to like him. He was gunning for anything that could make him quick money.

I want to buy a car, he said.

I could loan you some money when I have been paid.

That's a sweetie. I'll always be here for you.

Tani smiled girlishly.

I really like you, you know, he said.

Thank you. The smile widened.

I hope your husband doesn't mind?

Don't worry about him. He's a senile fool.

I wish I had been the one who married you.

Tani's heart skipped a beat. She wanted to keep him on the side; she wanted him to be there when she needed him. Lokons continued to visit her. She hadn't been paid the money she was waiting for, but she had borrowed some money to complete the building, which now stood waiting for her. Her confidence surged and nothing felt beyond her power. When she told

Lokons that she had a house, he kept coming even more assiduously. Maja complained and grunted, but there was nothing he could do. Tani hadn't time for him or the children, but she feared Ayimola because she could never fathom what was going on in his mind. She wanted to get out and be free.

Lokons came again one evening and Tani talked to him for more than three hours. Maja got angry when he saw she wasn't making any plans for dinner. At first he didn't say anything, he just kept coming and going out of the living room, slamming the door as he did so. Tani completely ignored him, which made matters worse.

Are you going to make dinner tonight? He said finally when he couldn't bear it any longer.

You must think I'm no more than your slave!

But that's one of your duties as a wife.

I think you ought to seriously start thinking about getting the services of a female slave.

Why are you so stubborn?

Why are you so foolish?

Watch your mouth!

Watch your mouth, too!

What kind of trouble is this? A man can no longer eat in his own house!

Have you got a house?

That's none of your business. I only want to eat my dinner.

And I've told you to get a slave.

Maja got really angry and asked Lokons to leave. The young man left very quickly and Tani became even more annoyed.

I thought you were a bit civilised. You're just a bloody old swine.

Watch your mouth, Tani.

You too watch what you do! How could you send the poor young man away like that? Who do you think you are? During my sister's wedding, what did you do? You were so useless. You ought to find out what other men, real men do when their wives' sisters are getting married. They move the heavens. They move mountains. But what did you do? Now you want to start dictating terms. You should be ashamed of yourself. That boy you've just sent away was one of the movers of the wedding reception and instead of you allowing me to show my appreciation, you sent him away. Ayimola must get to hear this. I'm really sick of it all.

Tani went on spluttering in anger. Maja drew close and struck her across the face. She started to yell and her children ran out of their bedroom to console her. Lokoma dragged her away and came back to hold Maja from inflicting more blows on her mother. The girl knelt before him pleading. Lines of spittle were dribbling out of the corners of his mouth. Tani was blinded by tears and wailed on. Sukuma didn't know what precisely to do, but he kept pleading half-heartedly with Maja, as his sister had instructed him. Ayimola wasn't at home and Lokoma was really terrified with the way Tani slumped on the bed when she took her inside. Her arms, too, had fallen limply. Maja stood in the corridor, shaking with rage and bawling out his lungs.

You are a witch! Nothing but a witch. I should have known, they warned me, I thought I should help hold my brother's family together and now you want to kill me. But I'll kill you first. I'll beat the hell out of you. Nothing but a whore. You're just a two-bit slut with a murderous instinct. That's what's taken you this far. Witch! Witch! Witch!

Please, sir, calm down don't listen to her anymore, said Lokoma dragging him away. She wished Otabolo was in but he had taken his day off. Tani went on crying in her room and hurling invectives at Maja from time to time. Maja would run up to her door and shout out his own stream of abuse.

You killed Solomon! We know that! Don't think because we haven't really said anything we don't know what happened. We know, you whore! You witch. We know and you'll soon get your retribution. You killed Solomon. You left him to die in penury after you had sucked him dry. God will get you for that. Don't think you will get off scot free. Everyone knows what is happening. We've only been keeping silent!

A while later, when things had begun to settle down, Ayimola returned. Lokoma let him in and whispered eagerly that Tani and Maja had had a violent quarrel. He breezed in and walked right into the living room, where he found Maja cooling off with a bottle of beer. Ayimola knew that it wasn't wise to ask him what happened. Maja could conceive it as rudeness. He greeted the old man and sat down as if he wasn't aware that anything had occurred.

Talk to that woman, talk to her, she's got to change, Maja said as Ayimola was settling into an armchair.

What happened?

Oh, it's a little matter. She's just got to be more diligent in her duties as a housewife.

Ayimola waited to see if more information would be divulged. But Maja remained uncommunicative, so Ayimola got up to go into his bedroom.

The following morning, Maja woke him up to ask if he had seen Tani and the kids.

No, I haven't left my room this morning.

Then where would they have gone?

Gone? How do you mean?

He followed Maja into Tani's bedroom. It was bare and there were signs that she had left hurriedly. The children's room was also in a similar state of disarray. Maja sank onto the floor in the corridor and started to cry helplessly. He looked hopeless.

Yes, they've left, Ayimola nodded pensively.

Oh, what kind of woman is this? What kind of a life? How could she just go like that? What have I done?

Ayimola turned to go into the sitting room.

Are you too leaving me?

Ayimola stopped. Hesitating, he returned and walked back to where the old man sat with his hands on his head, crying. He looked into his mouth and saw black holes everywhere. He had very few teeth left. His face looked pathetic, ludicrous, but Ayimola couldn't laugh. He couldn't laugh at the shrivelled, wailing mouth. He watched the hole that emitted funny, strange sounds until it ceased. He didn't have any words for Maja. Nothing could have diminished him more than to offer a piece of advice. Matters had gone beyond that. He looked at the old man's body and concluded he might still be able to throw a passable punch.

At sunset, Ayimola walked towards Henrietta's home. He had kept his promise not to drop in for a while. The flat seemed very quiet as he ascended the staircase. Georgina opened the door. She stood in the doorway as if to prevent him from entering, but he gingerly pushed his way inside the living room. The paintings and the masks were gone and the light was very dim. Ayimola spent some time asking about how Georgina was, to set her at ease, but it wasn't effective.

Where's Henrietta? he said finally.

She's gone.

Gone where?

Haven't you heard? Didn't she tell you?

No.

She left for Paris.

With the kids?

Yes.

When is she coming back?

We don't know.

He stood there, perplexed. A world seemed to have vanished just like that. A world that could have reinvented him, but he had shrunk from it, afraid of its immense power. Georgina's face seemed bland, somewhat indifferent. He looked at her legs, they were lovely in the miniskirt she had on. Her skimpy T-shirt spoke volumes. For the first time, he had really looked at her and he shuddered inside. He felt Henrietta's unbending presence everywhere and turned perfunctorily towards the door.

Printed in the United States
By Bookmasters